Clydesdale

MOVES TO ESSEX PARK

First Edition

Published by The Nazca Plains Corporation
Las Vegas, Nevada
2010

ISBN: 978-1-61098-017-3
E-book: 978-1-61098-018-0

Published by

The Nazca Plains Corporation ®
4640 Paradise Rd, Suite 141
Las Vegas NV 89109-8000

PUBLISHER'S NOTE
Clydesdale Moves to Essex Park is a work of fiction created wholly by *Bob Archman's* imagination. All characters are fictional and any resemblance to any persons living or deceased is purely by accident. No portion of this book reflects any real person or events.

Male Photo, Christopher Howey
Farm Photo, Jeecis

Art Director,
Blake Stephens

Clydesdale
MOVES TO ESSEX PARK

First Edition

Bob Archman

Part I

I've always looked older than my age. I was shaving by age 13 and bald by 18. I never looked young, but as I got older my looks stabilized. When I went to a good barber, a good haircut and a trimmed beard could make me look a little like Czar Nicholas. With a Fu Manchu and a ponytail, I became your basic redneck nobody. I was careful to keep a low profile, and never got my picture in the papers. I liked to work undercover and this suited me fine.

Clydesdale & Company kept a low profile, and this suited me fine. Most of the time we played back up for the run of the mill security companies. Most of these provided security guards for malls and residential complexes in Richmond. When they encountered something unusual, they would call us in.

I was surprised when Billy Fillmore dropped by. He had never used us. He thought his company, The Fillmore Group, was more than capable of handling things on their own.

"I've got a problem," he said. "Or at least I think it's a problem. We handle security for Essex Park."

"That's the wealthy and exclusive retirement community in New Essex County, isn't it?" I asked.

"That's it." he replied. "It's fenced and has security guards. Anyone under 35 stands out like a sore thumb unless they're wearing the development's uniform. There is no crime."

"So why are you here?"

"Most of my men are old codgers, retired army or police men types," he explained. "They get to know the residents well. A year or two ago one of the residents died and left an estate that was a lot smaller than my men had expected. They chalked it up to a misunderstanding. Last year another one died and the deceased left her children way less than they expected. A lot less. This year two more residents left disappointed family members."

"Lots of people are disappointed by wills," I said. "Maybe the kids weren't as nice to mom as they should have been. I think some people use it for revenge beyond the grave."

"In two of the cases my men knew the parent and the children well," Billy continued. "They seemed to be particularly close and devoted. All of the deceased were borderline Alzheimer patients. They were in the early stages of dementia, but not completely gone."

"Who runs the place?" I asked.

"That's what worries me," Billy said. "I mentioned my unease to the Executive director, Jon Dustin. He told me to forget it. When I persisted, he mentioned he might be looking at another security service. I got the message."

"Is he worried about bad publicity?"

"That might be part of it, but he's sort of the easy going, social butterfly type," Billy said. "He's worried about something. I was hoping you might take a gander at the place."

"How much money are we talking about?"

"In terms of cash on hand, the numbers aren't too large," Billy said. "One of the heirs said there had been some quite large checks made out to art galleries, but there were no new paintings in the apartments. One of my men is into art and he knows there were no signs of a $40,000.00 painting in the unit when he visited. Normally UPS and Fed-Ex deliver packages to the gate and my men deliver them. There have also been checks made out to consultants."

"Consultants can charge a lot," I remarked.

"Everyone who visits Essex Park must sign in and tell who they are visiting," Billy said. "The place is boring as shit. My men know if someone unusual drops in. There were no consultant types visiting. The only exception to the check in rules is for persons who come with senior staff members."

"You're thinking someone inside Essex Park may have a consultant's costume in their locker?" I asked. Billy nodded.

We talked and I agreed to join his operation as a maintenance man. Billy had a connection with the head of grounds and I would be working for him. I would see what I could sniff out. A week later, I was going through the gates of Essex Park. It was halfway between Richmond and Fredericksburg and somewhat isolated. The property was formerly a 1000-acre plantation and the development sat in the middle of the property. The original plantation house was now the clubhouse. The out buildings were converted into service uses and a recreational center. The security and staff lockers were housed in a small barn like building next to the infirmary. The development had a nurse on 24-hour call.

I was a grounds keeper and put in charge of pruning. I did this for my mother and Aunts and was good at it. This was a good way to get to know the residents. They were of an age that appreciated a well-trimmed bush. I am also Anglo, while most of the grounds staff was Mexican. The residents liked English-speaking men.

There was a staff locker room and showers. Everyone used an official Essex Park Uniform provided by the development. If you got dirty during the course of the day, you were expected to change. Sweat had to fresh to be acceptable. It was that sort of a development.

The upper level staff wore blazers, the rest of the staff wore polo shirts emblazoned with the Essex Park seal and shorts. I knew the residents were security oriented and there was no way to hide stolen objects in the uniform. This worked out well for me. While I couldn't carry off the family silver, I couldn't hide my family jewels either. Everyone soon knew I was well hung. A big cock can be an icebreaker for many men. I like to get to meet people as soon as possible.

I was wondering who would be the first to snap at the bait. I was a bit surprised when it turned out to be the daytime nurse, a beefy and butch man named Glenn. He shared the same locker room, but wore whites, rather than development colors of deep green shirts with khaki shorts.

We both started work at 8:00 and arrived a half hour early. Everyone else got there five or ten minutes early with just enough time to change. The first day he just looked at me. He wasn't what you would call an outgoing guy. That evening when we left he had seen me dirty, sweaty and with my bulge. The next day he was clearly looking me over.

On the third day we talked. We both lived in Richmond and he suggested we might car pool. It was a thirty-mile drive and the gas was costing us. He warmed up a lot. That evening he was held up with a patient. I hung around until he returned. Glen was surprised but pleased to see me.

"You're working late," he remarked.

4

"I bit off more than I could chew when I trimmed one of those big boxwoods. I had the trimming done by quitting time, but the cleanup took longer than I thought it would," I said. "You can see the brush from the plantation house and I know the residents would complain."

"They do like to complain, don't they?" Glenn asked as I stripped off my Essex Park clothes. We were alone in the locker room.

"You've got a beauty there," he said as he stared at my cock. "I've got a nice one, but it's nothing like yours."

"It's pretty, ain't it," I remarked. "It really does the trick if you've got an itch in a hard to reach place."

Glenn smiled at me. "Big balls too. Filled up?"

I smiled at him and looked around. "It's a bit public here," I remarked.

"I know a place," Glenn said. "Follow me."

We went to the corner of the locker room and he unlocked a door I hadn't noticed before. There was a small lounge area with a bed on one side. "This was originally planned to be the woman's lounge. This was for the PMS crowd. The women didn't want to share a locker room with men so they moved the lounge, but left the room. It's a party room for the executive director. He likes boys."

"He's not going to drop in, is he?"

"He's long gone. This is his golf night," Glenn said. He was transfixed as he stared at my cock. I peeled the skin back and exposed my head.

"Are you just a looker, or are you a man of action?" I asked. "If this is going to be a show and tell, I'd sure like to see what you have to show." Glenn stripped off his scrub shirt and exposed his barrel chest. He was stocky, but muscular. He had short stubble of hair on his chest. He must have shaved his body and it was growing back. He hesitated.

5

"Let's not stop short of the main attraction," I said. Glenn dropped his pants. I was afraid he hesitated because he wasn't as endowed much as me. He was uncut and a keeper, with a thick, six-inch tube dangling from his crotch. I dropped to my knees and took the soft tube of flesh in my mouth. It took me a whole two or three seconds to get him hard. If you could get whiplash from a guy getting hard, I'd have gotten it.

His body was massive compared to mine. Glen reached over and picked me up. He turned me upside down so I could suck him while he sucked me. I sucked his cock deep into my throat, as he tried to take all of mine. He didn't get all of it, but he did get a lot. Glenn moved over to the bed and we lay down. He didn't have much precum, but he was excited. I was getting turned on and he milked my drooling cock.

We stopped to get a breath of air. "I take it, you're a virgin," I asked.

He laughed. "I'm not exactly a virgin, but it's been a long while since I was this turned on," Glenn said. "I've been in a drought, and the little I've been getting hasn't come close to quenching my thirst"

"The executive director?"

"Let's just say he's not going to give King Kong a run for his money," Glenn replied. "He's not my type, and I'm not his."

"Am I your type?"

"With that cock of yours, you'd be my type if you looked like Pee Wee Herman," Glenn said. "I like my men to be men, not queens, or bois." He looked me in the eye. "I've never seen so much man in such a small package." He returned to sucking my cock. He was good at it and he soon got a mouthful of my sperm. I was shooting my second or third volley when he let loose.

When guys say they've been in a drought, that can mean almost anything. Either Glenn had the most productive balls in the world, or he'd been saving up. I got more than a mouth full. It was rich and creamy too. We broke apart and he looked at me. When he smiled, I saw his mouth was filled with my seed. We kissed and traded our man seed. As a kid, I was much impressed by Indians trading blood to become Blood brothers. Glen and I became sperm bothers.

I hate to think my cock does my thinking for me, but I trusted Glenn. His cock and my cock got along fine, as did our mouths and eventually our assholes.

He was still hard and drooling some, so after we kissed, I sat back and impaled myself on his cock. He was big, but not huge and it was a perfect fit. Glenn went a little crazy when I did that. I did a fancy dance on his love pole and then had a nice ride. After his earlier orgasm, I figured he was done, but damn if he didn't give my prostate a sperm bath. Then he buffed and polished my prostate until I popped for a second time. We were done for the night, but we agreed to car pool, just to insure we had an opportunity for a refill.

When I picked him up the next morning, we had a long chat in the car. Glen had some problems at his previous job and Essex Park was a distinct drop in status for him. There had been a bad divorce and some inappropriate photos had been found on his computer at the hospital where he worked. I also discovered he knew just about every resident at Essex Park and his or her medical problems.

He didn't like the executive Director much, but explained, "He's a wimp and ineffectual, but not a bad guy. He's good with the old ladies, and that's more than half the battle here. His boys are a different matter all together."

"What do you mean?"

"He likes the leach types," Glenn explained, "They flatter him and do his bidding, but a few of them are suspect in my view."

"Why do you think that?"

"I've got no facts, just suspicions," he said. "They're sweet as can be to the residents in public. They aren't so sweet in private. There are some difficult people here, but the boys can be really nasty. By the way, there are two guys here you might like,"

"Are these men who share our interests?" I asked.

Glenn nodded. "Captain Green in 12 Essex Park Crescent is a randy old sailor. He can still get it up and likes some fun. Bill Davis, the director of landscape services and your boss is a good guy too. He's surrounded by young guys all the time, but he likes men with more mileage. He's always looking for an outlet for his energy."

"How about an inlet?"

Glenn laughed. "I'm interested in the inlet part, but I'm not sure I can take it."

"You're tempted, but you're no fool?"

He laughed again. We reached Essex Park and went to our respective jobs. As it turned out I was working between units 11 and 12 of the Crescent. A thirty something man wearing an executive style Essex Park blazer was talking with an elderly lady on the deck to the rear of 11. The thirty something was oozing compliments to the clearly flattered woman. I could understand why Glenn wasn't pleased.

When the sun got higher, they went inside. I was trimming a hedge. My predecessor in the pruning job wasn't very good at it and I had to do a lot of remedial work.

"Aren't you shaving that bush a bit close?" a gruff voice asked. I looked up. A burly older man looked at me over the hedge.

"The bush was pruned the wrong way. If I don't trim it back, the upper part of the plant will shade the lower parts and it will get leggy," I said.

"Are you sure about that?"

"It the way my momma taught me how to do it." I replied. "She had the best hedges in town."

I glanced at him. He looked amused. The man was heavily tanned, with bright blue eyes and a white mustache. A thick mat of curly white chest hair poked out from his partially unbuttoned Hawaiian style shirt.

"I guess if your momma told you that, you should do it," he said. He went back to his house as I continued working on his hedge. Two hours later, I completed half of the hedge and it was looking good. The old man returned.

"Your momma was right," he said. "I'm sorry about butting in. I'm afraid I'm bored to tears here. Complaining and being a busybody is a way to pass the time."

I smiled. "You aren't the only one. One of the ladies gave me an ear full of instructions on trimming English Boxwood. I didn't tell her it was a Korean Holly," I said. The man looked me over. After two hours in the sun, I was dripping with sweat. My shirt and pants looked painted on. When his gaze got to my crotch, he did a double take. He looked up and saw I noticed him checking me out.

He laughed. "You can put a lot of eggs in that basket," he remarked.

"Two's enough for me," I said. "As long as I drain them regularly they fit just right."

"Are you offended by the curiosity?" he asked.

"Not at all," I said. "I'm used to it. Curiosity is natural." I looked him eye to eye. We understood each other.

9

"Why don't you drop by after work," he suggested. "We could have a beer. I'm Will Green, Captain Green, by the way." I said that sounded fine to me, but I told him I was car-pooling with Glenn, the nurse.

Green's face broke into a wide grin. "Bring him along. We're pals."

I went over to Green's house at five. Glenn was busy and said he'd come over when he was finished. Green was wearing a robe, he had been swimming at the club's pool. He offered me a beer and showed me the house. "If you are bored here, why are you here?" I asked.

"My late wife wanted to live in a quiet place. I was in intelligence. We had lived all over the world and she was a good sport about it, but she really didn't like it," he said. "It was her turn." In the living room there was a picture of a beautiful woman.

"Is that her? I asked.

"Yes. She was beautiful, but I was never sure she knew just how beautiful. She was simply a nice woman," he said. "She was a great help to a young naval officer on the rise. She never actually pushed me the way some officer's wives did."

"She didn't need to?"

He nodded. "She was shy, but naturally friendly and helpful. Everyone loved her," he said. "I'm aggressive and demanding. She softened the edges. Cancer got her two years ago."

"Sorry," I said. His gaze returned to my crotch. Out the window, I saw the man I had seen next door that morning was on the deck of the neighbors house drinking a glass of wine. "I didn't know the staff of Essex Park was that attentive. I saw that guy there this morning," I remarked.

"Lucy was hell on wheels when she came here, but she's been slipping," the Captain said. "They tend to pay attention to those who are slipping into La la-land. She was tight with the cash, but lately she's been spending money like water."

"Does she have the money to spend?"

"I would guess so," he remarked. "I've seen a few deliveries from an art gallery in Richmond. You can go through cash quickly if you move into art big time."

"She's interested in art?"

"That's what's been so funny," he mused. "We went to a few dinner parties there before my wife died. I would swear the place was furnished in straight department store furniture. No paintings at all, only photos of the family."

"Who is the man?"

"That's the director of Member Services, Henry Paulus," the Captain replied. "He's not my cup of tea. The assistant director, Eve Munson does all the work. He seems to spend his time buttering up old ladies." He stopped talking and looked at me. "I don't mind chatting, but I'd really like to have a fun roll in the hay. I was hoping you had the same interest?

"I take it you've been trying out the wild side?"

"I avoided a lot of things for my career and for my wife," he said. "I always had an interest, but lately I've been doing some exploring. Very successful exploring, I might add." His robe was tented a little, so I undid it. He was naked and his cock was at half-staff.

The Captain was beefy, hairy and a pretty good shape for a man of his age. "Let's go to the bed room and relax," he suggested. I took my shirt off as I walked. He was hot to trot and as soon as we were in the bedroom, he was at my cock. We soon were in the 69 position and that is where Glenn found us five or six minutes later.

Part 2

The Captain relaxed when Glenn appeared. They weren't just casual acquaintances. I think the Captain was fairly new to the gay scene and wasn't that comfortable meeting a new man. He clearly enjoyed men, but he still had his training wheels on. He was use to the well-ordered life of the military and was uneasy in the more free-wheeling gay community.

He knew Glenn and he let Glenn be his guide. Glenn was no virgin and seemed to have a good sense of what I liked and how far the Captain would go. The Captain had a nice, beer can style cock and matching meaty balls. Everything was in working order, but it did take a while to get the spigot flowing.

He was sucking Glenn and I was sucking him when the juices got going. It was worth the wait. His cock got hard and then came the flood. His cock juices didn't drool, they flowed. When the pre cum began to flow, it seemed as if his cock got more sensitive and responsive. I traded places with Glen and let the Captain suck me a second time. This time, he was enthusiastic.

When I get excited, eventually I want to fuck, but that wasn't to be. The Captain and Glenn shot off and things cooled down. We talked and the conversation turned to the widows. Widows were the majority of Essex Park residents. The Captain regarded them both as persons to be protected and as pests.

He was a big, strong and dominant man who naturally was protective, a classic Alpha male. He had no problem giving advice, or helping in medical or family emergencies, but he hated acting as the garbage man, or the yard boy.

"For some of the ladies a husband was just a personal servant," he complained. "Maybe they found a sucker the first time they married, but I'm no sucker. Some ask my advice as a form of entertainment, not because they really want it. Lucy wanted me for fun, but it seems that twerp, Henry Paulus, is the one whose advice she takes."

"I don't trust Paulus," Glenn said. "The old ladies get on everyone nerves once and a while, but I think he positively dislikes them. When I see him getting kissy-kissy with one of the residents, I get worried."

"You think he has ulterior motives?" I asked.

"I don't know anything at all, but I don't like it," he said. "He's not like Ira, the art director. He likes the old biddies."

"Ira's a flaming fagot," Captain Green said.

"Well, he is not going to give Clint Eastwood a run for the macho sweepstakes, but he is helpful," Glenn said. "He knows the ladies well enough to warn me if something's afoot. He told me Mrs. Taylor was looking pale. I checked on her and she was on the edge of a heart attack. He saw it coming."

"Maybe there's more to him than I noticed," Captain Green said. "His mannerisms drive me crazy."

"He can be one of the girls," Glenn conceded. "Ira does play the mother hen, but some of them need that. He watches over some of the ladies' medicines and makes sure they take it. He has a knack for that. They do what he tells them."

We had to get back, so Glenn and I left. That night I called my office and told them to do a background check on Henry Paulus and on the Director, Jon Dustin.

Early the next morning Glenn called. Ira, the art director's car had broken down. He wanted to know if I could pick him up. I said sure. He gave me the address. It was only a few blocks from where I lived.

Ira was the personification of mass media's idea of what a gay man should be. He was average height, slim and had a goatee. He was rather elegantly dressed in the Essex Park blazer. He embellished it with a scarf and gold necklaces. Ira talked a mile a minute and in a heavily lisped voice. He was not my type. If Ira wasn't my type, I was even less his. He likes young, smooth pretty boys, Asian if at all possible.

By the time I picked up Glenn and got to Essex Park, I realized Ira had a good sense of humor and was a well-informed gossip. He seemed to know each resident and his or her peculiarities. He was one of those persons who could meet a person and in ten minutes, he knew their birthday, their children's birthdays as well as what medications they were on. You find that in women regularly, but not in men. Ira was everything a detective could want.

I spent the day in general clean up. A bad thunderstorm had gone through in the early hours of the morning and limbs and leaves were down everywhere. I kept my eyes peeled for Henry and others of his ilk. I found him at one of the assisted living units. I get lucky regularly. My Mom thinks I'm God's favorite detective. Luckily, a big limb was down across the cul-de-sac from the unit he was visiting. It took more than an hour to clear it up.

About ten a big Mercedes drove up and a well-dressed couple got out. The man went to the trunk and got a package. It was rectangular and flat. My guess it was a framed painting or print. Henry greeted them at the door. Apparently, they were old friends. I got the license plate of the car. Later that day I saw Henry and a young woman visiting another unit. I got the unit's number and would talk with Glenn about it later.

I was driving around the place in a little lawn tractor with a trailer behind, to hold the branches. I could cover a lot of ground in that, so I got a good feel for the place. The Captain flagged me down to look at a branch in his patio. It was more of a twig than a branch.

"I have some friends in Richmond," he said. "They knew you and didn't know you did yard work."

"I have a lot of skills," I said. "If you didn't mention any of my other skills to the residents or staff, I'd appreciate it."

"Damn, I guessed right," he said. He looked pleased with himself. "Something's up! What is it?"

"It's a bit early yet," I replied. "Nothing is definite; there is just a faint odor in the air. You could say I'm still sniffing things out."

"I can keep a secret. I've had a few slightly uneasy feelings about this place. By the way, my friends in Richmond described you as a hairy chimp who is hung like King Kong," he added.

"Did they like the chimp part, or the hung part?"

Green smiled. "They knew about you and had heard about it," he said. "Apparently I've started at the top."

"Given my druthers, I'm a top," I said, smiling.

"I've never done that," he replied. "Glenn's interested, but I'm not sure. This is all uncharted territory for me. If I can help you on your investigation, I'm more than willing."

"That may work out," I said. "I may need some background on the residents when I figure out if something is amiss." I went back to my clean up tasks. I got beeped to go back to the house where I had cleaned up the large limb earlier. Another branch had fallen.

Henry Paulus was waiting for me. He had a put upon look. "Mrs. Anderson is very disturbed you didn't remove the branch that was going to fall," he said. "I don't like sloppy work like that." It was a silly thing to say, since the branch was still in the tree when I was there that morning, but I didn't say anything about that.

"I'll clean it up right away sir," I said. I could tell he wanted to huff and puff a bit longer, but I went to work right away and he didn't have a chance. He went back in the house. I made short work of the branch.

I went to the door and knocked. A maid answered the door. "I just took care of the downed branch," I said. "Are there any other trees down?"

"Come in," the maid replied. "I'll ask Mrs. Anderson." The entry faced directly into the living room. The packing for the painting was on the floor and a painting was in the wall behind the sofa. It was smaller than the painting that had been there before and you could see the light spot where the earlier painting had hung. The new painting was of a western scene in the style of Remington.

"Ask him to wait for a few minutes," I heard an aggravated voice say. "I'm busy now." The maid reappeared and gave me the message. She left and I took the opportunity to look at the painting and the wrapper. The wrapper had a label saying, the Miller Galleries of Americana. The address was 3212 Cary Street, Richmond. The painting was signed F. D. Remington, 1893. I didn't think it was a print, but it was either a good copy, or the real thing. It was either very expensive, or stunningly expensive, I was back in the entry by the time Mrs. Anderson appeared with Henry.

"What do you want here?" she asked. "You don't belong here!"

"This is the man who was removing the fallen limbs," Henry explained.

"What limbs?" she demanded. She looked enraged, and then she became confused, lost.

"Do you have anything else you want to have done?" I asked.

She looked around the room and saw the painting. "Who stole my painting?" she asked. "That's not my painting."

"That's the new painting you just bought, Betty," Henry said. He looked at me. "You'd better go." The maid opened the door and I heard her latch it behind me as I left.

I drove my lawn tractor to a shady spot and called into my office. Lewis, the office manager picked up the phone. "I need for someone to check out the Miller Galleries of Americana. It's an art gallery of some sort," I said. "Is there any information on Henry Paulus and Jon Dustin?"

"Let me check the file," Lewis said. He was silent for a few seconds as he pulled up the computer records. "Zip so far, but I just Googled The Miller galleries. Mostly self-generated promo stuff, but there is one news article. "Gallery Admits to Error in Attribution," is the title. It looks like they had a problem selling a painting with a forged signature. Is that the information you wanted?"

"We may have hit the jackpot," I said. "Who's our most likely art investigator now? Let's do a full investigation on the Miller Galleries."

"Gus is into that," Lewis said. "He moves in those circles. I'll get him on it right away."

What had been a faint suspicion that something was wrong had turned into a stench. The combination of wealthy elderly people slipping into their dotage and an unscrupulous art dealer selling suspect works could make for a great scam.

I was a know-it-all kid in High School and proud of being born a redneck. I explained his to my freshman English teacher, Mrs. Franken. She was a plump Jewish lady whose husband was a Doctor. "There's a world of difference between being a redneck and being an ignorant redneck," she said. "We're all born ignorant, but that's no reason to die ignorant."

I thought that was a put down at first, then I realized it was true. I've picked up a lot of knowledge since I was in Mrs. Franken's class. What chance was there that a genuine Frederick Remington would end up over the sofa in Mrs. Anderson's house? The chances had to be somewhere between zero and none.

It looked real to me. Forgers specialized in creating that "real" look. There was one other option. Perhaps the painting was real, but stolen. If I were going to hide a work of stolen art, Essex Park would be the ideal place. The attics and basements of art dealers in New York or Amsterdam would seem to be a likely hiding place. Mrs. Anderson's living room in rural Virginia would not.

On the drive home, I got the lowdown on Mrs. Anderson from Ira and Glenn. "To tell you the truth, if the word "bitch" hadn't been invented yet they would have had to make it up to describe her," Glenn said. "She's demanding, pretentious and totally self-centered."

"Actually Glenn is treating her kindly," Ira said. "The staff hates her as do the residents. She was trailer trash who married an elderly car dealer. He died and left her well off, but not that well off. I listened to her sound off on her hubby's children once. She wanted it all, but only got 33%. Talk about bitter."

"How big was the 33%?" I asked.

"I'm not sure, maybe a million, or a million and a half," Ira said. "She's comfortable, but not floating in cash."

"I take it, not many people gather around the Thanksgiving table at her house," I remarked.

"Somehow I think she may have an estranged daughter," Glenn said. "She had a knack for ruining dinner parties, so she doesn't get out much. That last time she came in to see me, she was slipping badly. I couldn't tell if it was dementia, or booze that was causing the problem."

"What did she come to see you about?" I asked.

"I can't talk about that. She's a patient," Glenn said. "She usually doesn't come to see a lowly nurse practitioner; she needs a doctor. If she had her druthers she'd have them flown in directly from the Mayo Clinic."

"Is she the arty type?"

"Shit no," Ira responded. "She's the Dollar General type. She can do Martha Stewart stuff since she's read about it, but that's as far as she can go. Her house was done by a decorator in Richmond. There were threats of lawsuits about that, but they never materialized. Betty hates lawyers." I dropped the men off and went home.

There was a message for me on the phone from Elliot Stevenson. He was the Curator of American art at the Museum. I called him back and he asked if I could come over to chat about the Miller galleries. I had a quick dinner and went to his Monument Avenue house. I had done some security work for the Museum so I was familiar with the museum and its staff.

I had seen Elliot several times. Elliot is a good six foot five inches tall. You always see Elliot. He looked like a caricature of a museum curator with a goatee and slightly affected mannerisms. I wouldn't say he was effeminate, but you would never mistake him for a longshoreman or a truck driver. He had encyclopedic knowledge about American art. He knew it all.

I was put off by him the first time I met him. He seemed like a pompous, know-it-all jerk. Later I discovered he did indeed know it all. He was just a bit light in the social skills.

"Why are you interested in the Miller galleries?" he asked. I explained the situation and told him about the Remington. He was interested in that. Elliot called a friend as asked him to come over. Five minutes later an aging hippie appeared at the door.

"Clydesdale, this is Sedgwick Montague, the head of the painting conservation lab at the museum," Elliot said in introduction.

"You are the famous Clydesdale, the horse hung detective?" Sedgwick asked. I smiled and we shook hands.

"Are you interested in the detective or horse hung part of me?" I asked. Poor Elliott looked scandalized. Sedgwick was disheveled and sloppy looking. He was bald, wore a ponytail and had a Blackbeard the Pirate style beard. He wore a paint splattered Hawaiian style shirt, only partially buttoned. It looked as if he tucked the beard into the shirt, but it was possible his chest hair was as thick as his beard. Elliott was thin and wore a Victorian style smoking jacket and an Ascot. He was perfectly groomed. That contrast between the two men was stunning.

"Can you tell me about the Remington?" Sedgwick asked. I went over the story again. They were more than interested.

"The Miller Galleries have been suspect for years, but they've been slippery." Elliott explained. "We almost got them once, but they talked themselves out of it."

"Are they forgers, or are they fencing?" I asked.

"They like to add signatures and dates to paintings that aren't quite so deserving," Sedgwick said. "It wouldn't surprise me if they worked with paintings of problematic provenance. I rather doubt they would take the artworks themselves. They are white-collar people; I don't think they are into dirty hands. "

"Does problematic provenance mean stolen from a Jewish family and formerly in the collection of Hermann Goering?" I asked.

"That's what it means, but there are many stolen works floating around," Elliot said. "Can you get us in to see the painting?"

"That my take some work, but I will see what can be done," I said. We talked for an hour or so. Elliott knew all about stolen works. Sedgwick covered the forgery front. I went home at 11:00. Sedgwick was right behind me.

"Do you have time for a night cap?" Sedgwick asked. He had run to catch up with me. "Elliot doesn't drink anything but expensive wine and he saves it for himself. It's his only vice."

"I don't need a drink, but here is another vice I wouldn't mind indulging," I said. "If you're a Bottom, that is."

"Did I just get lucky?" he asked. "My apartment is a block away. I have been known to entertain on the back porch."

"Are you a size queen?"

"Can I answer that later?" he asked.

Sedgwick may not have been a size queen when we met, but he was one two hours later. As soon as we got naked, I knew Sedgwick had an aesthetic admiration for my cock. Several men get that deer caught in the headlights look when they see it the first time. For Sedgwick it was as if he had discovered a new Rembrandt. He loved it as an object of beauty, a work of art. He studied it in detail then used his tongue to explore it.

Sedgwick possessed a classic fireplug cock. It was a six by six inch wonder. Once we got going, it flowed like a fire hydrant too. His cock was on the upper end of average; his balls were in the 90th percentile. He had bull balls dangling in a hairy, bull ball sack.

He told me his partner had left him for another man a year earlier. His partner was a top, but had a long thin cock that fit easily. He wanted my cock but wasn't sure he could take it. I got Sedgwick on his back with his legs spread wide. He had a pretty rosebud poking out of his hole. The second my lubricated knob touched the bud, he shivered and his ass hole opened.

I knew I'd have no problem. It wouldn't be easy, but he wanted it all. Sedgwick was tight, but he wanted it bad. I used a lot of lube and just pumped gently until my head popped the sphincter. Ten minutes later, my curly hairs touched his ravaged hole. Each inch of penetration was difficult, but after I slowed up for a few seconds, he'd beg me to go deeper. Deeper I went.

Sedgwick must have had a particularly sensitive ass. Once my cock stretched the hole, it became ultra-sensitive. Every movement I made caused him to react. Sometimes he would moan, shiver or twitch. By the time I got him fully skewered, he was crying. I stayed perfectly still until he got a grip. I moved and he shivered.

I pulled out to let him rest, then I rolled him over and did him doggy style. That was much easier. Once he got use to that I flipped him again and deep dicked him on the first thrust. I came damn close to shooting so I pulled out and rested. I figured that was enough fucking for one night.

I rested and felt drowsy. Sedgwick got up and went to the bath. He took a shower. When he returned he straddled me and sat on my cock. By now, his ass lips parted and welcomed my cock into his body, we merged. His ass was shrink-wrapped to my cock. It was lovely.

I had an odd vision of the Vulcan Mind Meld from Star Trek. It wasn't the mind that melded for Sedgwick and me; it was a cock-prostate merger. They formed a new, super sex organ we could share. He sat, impaled on my cock, twitching and moaning until I felt his entire ass contract. A second later, I was giving his prostate a sperm bath as his seed squirted from the slit and coated my hairy chest in cum.

Part 3

I left Sedgwick's apartment at one in the morning. I knew I was going to see him again. Glenn drove the next morning, so I got a little more sleep in the car. I don't need a lot of sleep anyway. While Sedgwick kept me up late, I sure was relaxed that morning.

I met Essex Park's director for the first time after work. Jon Dustin was short, slightly pudgy man who didn't strike me as a leader of men. Apparently, Henry had spoken to him about my work at Mrs. Anderson's house. Jon came to the locker room to talk with me, but ran into Glenn before he got there. Glenn set him straight; he also mentioned my endowment.

Glenn told me Jon was into twinks, but I guess he was willing to look at alternative forms of entertainment. I thought Jon used his position to get sexual favors, but when I met him, I realized that was unlikely. Jon was a timid and very careful pencil pusher. He was proper and almost prissy. His taste for pretty boys was his weakness. It was much more likely ambitious young men knew of his weakness and exploited them, than Jon was exploiting them for his sexual gratification. The locker room was empty, except for me. I emerged from the shower wearing only a towel.

I have a friend who says if I could just walk around naked all the time, I would be the most popular man in the world. Whatever Jon wanted to say to me about Mrs. Anderson was forgotten when he saw my cock. I'm small, but muscular and well built. I'm a fur ball and you can't see the muscles through the hair. Fortunately, my cock isn't covered in hair and it stands out.

You would think a man who likes pretty boys would be turned off by my type, but that underestimates the power of the cock. When I'm naked no one looks at my face. I could tell Jon didn't want to be seen looking, but he couldn't help himself. I spent a lot of time drying my hair, so he could have guilt free inspection time.

He asked me how much I liked working there and asked if I had any problems. This conversation went on for a few minutes. I made no effort to get dressed, and he made no effort to leave. Clearly, Jon was afraid to make the first move. For me it was a close your eyes and think of England situation. I wasn't too enthusiastic about sucking, or fucking him.

Another employee entered and I was off the hook. I got dressed and went to the car to wait for Glenn. Ira was already there. I mentioned that I had met Mrs. Anderson the day before and she was losing it. "Are there many here who are in the same situation?" I asked.

"There are always some in the twilight period," Ira said.

"Twilight?"

"That's when they are slipping, but not gone," Ira explained. "It's the most dangerous time for us. You think everything is fine, and then you find them barbecuing eggs over the back yard grill at three o'clock in the morning."

"That's a bad sign?"

Ira laughed. "The big problem is when they fry bacon for three hours and the alarms go off," Ira said. "The units all have fire alarms connected to the central office. The night guard, Lizzy Smith, is really good about keeping an eye on problem residents. She's the motherly type. When there are lights on at two in the morning, she checks it out. The transitional units don't have kitchens, but some residents can be very creative when it comes to a hot plate or a coffee maker."

"Is there someone in charge of the borderline residents?"

"There is, but it's an odd choice of staff," Ira said. "Paulus is one of them and Tiffany Lewis is the other. She is the Recreation director. Neither of them seems to like the old folks much, but they like the ones that are slipping."

"Maybe it inspires their sense of charity?"

"If you met them, you would know how unlikely that is," Ira said. "Both seem to be entirely self-centered." Glenn arrived and we went back to Richmond. I had several reports waiting at the office. Jon Dustin was an ordained Baptist minister who had a congregation at one time. His wife apparently discovered his little secret and wanted to use it in a divorce proceeding. He resigned and took the administrative job at Essex Park. He lived modestly and was regarded as an exemplary pencil pusher. By all accounts, he was well respected, but not much liked.

Henry Paulus was a man on the make. He had been through a number of jobs, never staying in one place for more than 18 months, until he arrived at Essex Park. He had been there for three years. He drove an old Dodge to work, but there was a Jaguar parked in front of his expensive condominium in Richmond. His former employers were carefully non-committal about his work. That usually meant they were afraid of him taking legal action if they gave him a bad recommendation.

Henry also had a live in. The houseboy was a 22-year-old Mexican named Julio. My operative discovered there had been a series of young men. Apparently, age 23 the cut off age. He would ditch them and replace them with someone younger. He liked Asians who looked younger than their years. Julio was an exception to the string of Asian boy toys.

I called Clint, the operative who made the report. "Reading between the lines, I take it you weren't much impressed by Henry Paulus?" I said.

"Well he ain't my cup of tea, that's for sure," Clint said. Clint was a native of Galax, Virginia. He liked his men manly. "I just discovered something interesting. He definitely lives above his means, but I ran into Randy Butler, the Realtor who sold Paulus his condo. Paulus paid in cash, $550,000.00."

"An inheritance maybe?"

"His parents live in a trailer in Orlando. His dad is retired, but works as night guard at a local hospital to get a little extra money," Clint explained. "I don't think he comes from money. His salary at Essex Park is about $45,000.00 a year."

"Any other bombshells?"

"As a matter of fact, yes." Clint said. "Apparently his residence of record is a house off Jefferson Davis Highway. He owns a rancher there. He rents it out, but that is where Essex Park thinks he lives. It's also where the Commonwealth of Virginia thinks he lives. It's not in the worst part of Jefferson Davis, but nothing on the road is of any account."

"By the way, how did you run into Randy?" I asked. "He's a bit high toned for you, isn't he?"

"It was at his birthday party."

"Were you in the cake?"

"I wasn't exactly in the cake. I was sort of a birthday present for him."

"How did it work out?"

"Unexpectedly good. One of his friends thought he'd like me. He did, but I liked him too. Let's just say I didn't know I could shoot off five times on one night. His ass was so full of my cum it was coming out of his ears."

I called Gus, my art man next and asked about the Miller Galleries of Americana. Gus was a sculptor who had been making ends meet by working as a guard for one for the security companies we worked for. He helped us with a case and we hired him for some of our arty clients. We did security for art exhibits and galleries and he could fit in with the crowd. He was the perfect plain-clothes man for those occasions.

"Miller is on the outer edge of respectability," Gus said. "For years they sold Wild West Pictures and Civil War paintings. About five years ago, they began moving in to more mainstream artists. They sold a painting by Thomas Eakins to a local collector. He made the mistake of giving it to the museum and it turned out to be a forgery. The portrait was by an adequate late Nineteenth Century artist, but the signature was forged. When the museum cleaned it, the forgery was discovered."

"Was the conservator Sedgwick Montague?"

"It was," Gus said. "Do you know him? He's a character. Sharp as a tack, but a character."

"I just met him," I said. "It caused a stink?"

"Oh yes. The Gallery had to give back the cost of the painting," Gus said. "It was only $100,000.00 which is dirt cheap for an Eakins. The purchaser knew that. He planned to get a tax break when he gave it to the museum listing the painting at the full market value. They were lucky the IRS didn't find out about it. There was potential fraud involved."

"What would the value of an Eakins be?" I asked. I wasn't familiar with the artist.

"The Gross Clinic went to the Philadelphia Museum for $65,000,000.00. The Miller Eakins wasn't a major painting, but had it been an Eakins, it would be hard to think of it going for less than a million," Gus explained. "There aren't a lot of them floating around."

"So the gallery is selling big names at a bargain price?"

"That seems to be what they are doing," Gus replied. "They aren't selling to the big time collectors. They market to nouveau riche, or uninformed collectors. They have been keeping under the radar lately."

"Have you ever heard of a man named Henry Paulus?"

"Nope, never met him." Gus answered. Gus went on to explain the suspicions about the Gallery. "Unfortunately, they are all unproven suspicions as of now."

I went to bed early and recharged my batteries. I was tired from both my return to manual labor and my long night with Sedgwick. I picked up Ira and Glenn the next morning and went to work. I did get a few names of residents who were slipping from Ira

Ira contacted me during the day and said he had to stay late to teach a class. The person who was supposed to teach it had called in sick. I said I didn't mind staying late if it was okay with Glenn. Ira checked with Glenn and he was fine. Glenn always had paperwork he could do.

I got to the employee locker room at six. I noticed Jon was in Glenn's office with a third man. Somehow, I had a feeling they were waiting for me. As I walked by, Glenn waved at me to come in.

"Willy, come join us we're all here late today," Glenn said. I was using my real name, Wildridge, not Clydesdale at Essex Park. "You know Jon, this is Larry. "He's an intern here as part of his MBA program.

Larry was 23 or 24, a little short of six feet tall and almost pretty. He was slim and very elegant. He had curly black hair, a trimmed beard and beautiful pale blue eyes. Our eyes met and I saw curiosity and lust in his eyes. He saw only lust in my eyes.

"You're learning the ropes of Retirement Communities?" I asked.

Larry smiled, "It's a growth industry. There's going to be need for thousands of these places over the next decade."

I was sweaty and dirty. I caught a whiff of myself. "I need to take a shower if we're going to have a civilized conversation here," I said. "Can excuse me for a few minutes?"

"Why don't you use the executive shower here," Larry asked. "I could use a shower too. Are you the shy type?" While Jon looked nervous as hell, Larry wasn't the shy type at all. I guessed no one had ever passed up a shower with him. Glenn looked amused.

"Not at all," I relied. "Everyone has the same equipment." Glenn got up, locked the door and turned off the lights. We adjourned to the shower. When we stripped, Larry made no effort to disguise his interest. The shower was large. Apparently, it had been a small room and they tiled the entire space when they converted it to a shower. Larry and I went in and got the water going.

One nice thing about younger guys is that get hard easily. Larry had a nice seven-inch cock that curved toward his navel. The shaft was thin, but the knob was large and cut. He had pale white skin, his chest was covered is silky black hair. The only color was his pink lips and tits, blue eyes and lavender cock head. He was beautiful.

"You have to be the ugliest man I've ever seen," he said. "I don't think I've ever been this turned on. You're uncut too. I've never played with an uncut one before."

31

I was firming up a little, but the skin still covered my head. I was wondering what a lavender cock head tasted like when he decided to do some foreskin exploration. I had showered that morning, but it had been a hot day and I hadn't had the opportunity to peel back the skin and air it out. I was afraid it might be a baptism of fire for a guy sucking his first uncut meat.

I didn't need to worry. Since I was still soft, he took my entire organ into his mouth. He sucked it in, pulling as much skin into his mouth as he could. With all the extra skin in his mouth, he worked his tongue into the pucker and tongue fucked my foreskin. I didn't stay soft for long. The tip of his tongue and the tip of my cock met. As luck would have it, he found my slit. I must have been oozing some, because he lingered at the slit. He flicked his tongue at the slit to sample my balls juices before he explored the rest of my knob. He knew the sensitive places on a cock head. As I said before, Larry wasn't shy and he wasn't a virgin.

By then Glenn and Jon were in the shower with us. Jon was slightly overweight and not at all toned. He looked embarrassed. He was not so embarrassed as to lose his erection. It was a good cock. I had a friend who referred to cocks like his as standard issue.

"I'm in the land of the giants," he said.

Glenn smiled at him. "It's not what you have, but what you do with what you have that matters," he said. Jon dropped to his knees and sucked on Glenn's erect cock.

I soon discovered Jon's strong suit was cock sucking. He loved it. Jon wanted cock, he didn't want any reciprocation; he just wanted to suck. That was good for all of us. I discovered he had the shortest fuse of any man I had ever met.

Larry later told me it was part of Jon's Baptist upbringing. He thought his body was a temple, and he wanted to keep it pure. Jon seems to have had an odd interpretation of the biblical quote that it wasn't what you put in your mouth, but what comes out of it. Cock and cum were fine, he just wanted his cock and ass left untouched.

I always like to give as much as I take, but Jon was happy and we were happy. He sucked and sucked and sucked and never got tired. I don't know what he did, but Jon had a magic tongue. It was delicate and surprisingly effective.

Larry looked as if he might be delicate, but he had the sexual stamina and drive of a bull. He liked oral. He liked anal and if you could have fucked his nose, he'd have liked nasal. When Jon sucked me, Larry went off to suck and then fuck Glenn. Glenn wanted to be fucked, but he wasn't a natural bottom. I didn't know if his ass was tight, or if he couldn't relax enough to open up for Larry.

Larry liked a challenge. He was a hard, but fair fucker. He took his time, but never took his eyes off the prize. He knew Glenn really wanted it, and eventually he got it. Glenn was happy. Larry kept his eyes on my cock as Jon worked it over. As he deep dicked Glenn he looked at me. "Do you like to fuck?" he asked.

I nodded. "I top," I replied. Larry smiled as he rammed Glenn hard. Glenn was on his hands and knees, taking it doggy style. He moaned and reared up. He sprayed the shower room with sperm. Larry continued to pump slowly then pulled out. He was still hard and his lavender cock head was now a deep purple.

Jon had stopped sucking, so he watched Glenn shoot off. He scooted over to lick up the cum still drooling from Glenn's cock.

Larry came over to me. "Do you think you can take it?" I asked.

"I'm not sure, but I want to try," he said.

"Have you taken a big one before?" I whispered.

"No, nothing like yours," Larry replied. He leaned close to me. "I've liked getting fucked a lot, but I've always had the feeling that a bigger one would be better. It's like an itch that's deeper than anyone's been able to scratch."

Glenn had recovered from his orgasm and came over to us. "If you don't mind, I'd love to watch," he said.

"I like an audience," Larry said. I smiled and Jon looked like he had died and gone to heaven.

We were still in the shower, so we dried off and went to the next room. It had a cot.

Glen had stocked the room with some lube. "I wish I had some poppers," Glenn said. "A little bit of sugar makes the medicine go down."

"What are poppers?" Jon asked.

"I'll explain latter," Glenn said.

"I just got back from a vacation in Amsterdam," Larry said. "I have an unopened bottle of high test." He produced a small blue bottle. "Do you want a snort now?" he asked, offering me the bottle.

"Not now," I said. "Let's save it for the rough spots. Glenn can you lubricate Larry's ass? Jon, would you like to slobber up my cock?" Jon was more than willing.

Glenn got Larry on his back and worked some lube into the young man's ass. Larry loved it and I mean loved it. Then Glenn got something that looked a bit like a small turkey baster. He filled it with lubricant and inserted it in Larry's hole. As he pulled it out, he injected the lube, filling Larry's entire love tunnel. He then worked on the hole itself. He started with one finger, added a second, then a third. Larry was opened and ready for fun.

Jon was going to town on my cock. "Juice it up really good," I told him. "Slobber over it. I want it to slip in easy. It may be messy, but it will go in easy!"

When Glenn got his fourth finger in Larry's hole, it was time. Glenn had Larry's legs bent over his chest so the ass was open and defenseless. Glenn pulled his fingers out. Larry's sphincter didn't have time to close before my cock head was on the dark side of the ring of muscle. A second later, his ass swallowed my entire cock. His eyes rolled back into his head and he moaned. To this day I don't know if I pushed in, or he sucked me in. usually I let a guy recover after full penetration, but Larry didn't need that. I began slowly thrusting. It was fine. Glenn opened the poppers, gave Larry a snort, and then held the bottle to my nose. I took a deep snort. The fumes hit him a second or two before they hit me. There was no way either of us could hold back.

He craved my cock, I had an urge to get deeper and deeper into his guts. We lasted about five minutes of incredibly intense sex then he and I shot off together. Much to my surprise Jon was there eating up Larry's cum as it squirted from the bloated cock.

I pulled out as my ejaculations diminished, but Jon kept on sucking Larry's meat, taking everything that Larry's balls could produce. When he got up, Larry's hand touched Jon's cock and he climaxed. Jon had a short fuse, but a full load. Glenn had leaned over to lick the last drips from Larry's cock and was therefore able to take Jon's cum. Glenn looked up when he felt the first splatter, opened his mouth and Jon filled it. Robin Hood never hit a target as accurately as Jon hit Glenn's mouth.

Glenn swallowed Jon's meat in one gulp. When the major ejaculations stopped, he continued to suck until he suctioned the last drops of man seed from Jon's balls. Jon was moaning in pleasure. From time to time, he shivered when he had another ejaculation. Jon was drained, but had a blissful look on his face.

Glenn was still hard and excited. After coating his cock in lube he said, "Jon, I know you think you don't want this, but I know better." Glen lifted Jon's legs and buried his cock in Jon's virgin ass. Jon was totally unprepared and relaxed. He moaned at the nurse's organ filled him. "I'm going to plow your ass and do some seeding!" Glenn proclaimed.

Glen screwed him for ten minutes and he shot off. When he pulled out, Larry had recovered enough to take his place. Jon loved young men and he was in heaven. When Larry popped and pulled out, Jon's hole remained dilated and I filled it. I didn't actually fuck Jon. I just slipped my cock in his ass and rested. His hole closed on my member. John sighed. This may sound odd, but his ass was cozy.

"You may have the biggest cock you will ever take in you now," Glen said, "Are you okay?" Jon nodded. He was dazed. I don't think he knew sex could be that good. He didn't move. I shifted a little and Jon's erupted in a massive orgasm. His ass twitched and that was good for my cock. It may sound stupid, but I like watching an uptight man shoot the load of his lifetime. At least he could go to his maker knowing how good things could be.

When I pulled out, Glenn and Larry's cum drooled from his ass. We showered and dressed. As we left, he whispered to me, "Can anyone tell what I've done?"

I smiled. "Not at all." Jon smiled.

Part 4

The evening had one other benefit. Larry joined our car pool. Ira's car was fixed, so he decided to drive alone. With gas prices what they are, car-pooling made sense to Larry. To tell you the truth I think Jon would have joined if he could. Jon was an odd case. My gut reaction was that he wasn't involved. He wasn't a leader of men and he wasn't a user. It was easy to see a character like Henry using him. I don't think Jon was able to resist an aggressive man.

As we drove to work the next day, I asked Larry how he connected with Jon. Larry was an open book. When I was his age, I was worried about being gay and kept it secret. That hadn't occurred to Larry. "Henry told me Jon liked some fun on the side," Larry said. "Henry claimed once Jon had sucked your cock, he was yours. Apparently once he's sucked you, he gets paranoid you'll tell and he's pretty much under your control."

"Do you control him?" Glenn asked.

"Shit no," Larry said. "I can get where I want to go without blow jobs lubricating the way."

"Why did you do it, then?" I asked.

"To put him out of his misery," Larry replied, "He wanted it so bad, I felt sorry for him. Oddly, Henry didn't tell me Jon was the Michelangelo of cocksuckers. Jon's not my type, but he's fun and there are no strings."

"Are we charity cases too?" Glenn asked.

"You men are 90% pure, unadulterated lust and 10% exploration," Larry replied. "I've never been with older men, and never with guys like you. I attract handsome men like a magnet. When I was younger, I was popular with the men at my parents' country club. I could pick and choose who I wanted, so I avoided the older guys."

"So last night was slumming?" I asked.

"That's what I thought it would be," Larry said. "I thought it might be interesting. I had no idea I would be so turned on. I also had no idea I would get to totally fucked. Totally fucked in a nice way, that is."

"How is your asshole?" Glenn asked.

"A little tender, but it's my brain that got fucked," he said.

"Will's cock isn't that long!" Glenn said.

"Well it is," Larry said. "I've never been finger fucked like the way you did it either. I've had an index finger and a few cocks in my ass before, but nothing like last night. I was riding a tricycle and suddenly found myself riding a Harley. "

"You're okay?" I asked.

"I sure am," Larry replied with enthusiasm. "I loved it. I thought I knew all about man sex. It seems I have just barely scratched the surface. That's what I mean when I said Will fucked my brain. I need to do some rethinking about what sex is and with whom I want to have sex. What I had thought was hot and heavy sex turned out to be more of a Sunday School picnic."

It was possible Larry was involved in the swindle, but he struck me as being self-confident and self-assured. He didn't need a scam to be successful. Henry was a different man all together. I had people looking into his life and guessed it would not be pretty.

It appeared forged paintings were involved. I wasn't sure how they worked into the fraud. It seemed very complex. Some elderly residents at Essex Park paid big bucks for forged paintings. Somehow, Henry could pay $500,000.00 cash for a condo. I had no idea what the link was. I knew about one suspect painting, the Frederick Remington, and I didn't know if there were others.

It was a quiet day at Essex Park, so I went by to see the Captain. I trimmed several shrubs to the rear of his unit. He appeared a few minutes later.

"You sure keep this place looking good," he said.

"I do my best," I said. "It's hot today."

The Captain was a smart man. He knew what I wanted. "Come on in and get a drink," he said.

When I got in the kitchen, we could talk. "This may sound a little odd, but have you noticed any of your neighbors buying paintings?"

"No I haven't, but I haven't been looking either," he said. "Who are you thinking about?"

"I happened to be in Mrs. Anderson's house," I said. "She had a Frederick Remington hanging over the sofa."

"That's unlikely," the Captain said. "She has no interest in art at all. She has money, but not that kind of money."

"Are you interested in art?" I asked.

"I wasn't, but my wife was," he said. "I pretended to like it just to humor her and I got hooked. I'm afraid nautical scenes and seascapes appeal to me. My tastes aren't sophisticated. I have several good paintings, but even the second tier talents are pricey. A real Remington is almost impossible for a normal wealthy collector. You need to be a billionaire."

"Do you think you might drop in and visit a few people and see if they might have something new hanging on the wall?" I asked.

"Who are you thinking about?" he asked. I gave him a list of several of the residents Ira had mentioned as borderline.

"They are all going gaga," he said. I nodded. "I see, maybe I'll have a little cocktail party tomorrow and ask them in person."

"That would be nice," I said. "I'd better get back to work."

That evening the Captain just happened to be walking by the locker building and he waved at me. I went over to see him.

"You were right," he said. "Three of the residents had nothing new, or were too far gone to make any sense. Ellen Smith and Emily Carlisle both had recently invested in a painting. Ellen had a small Mary Cassatt portrait of a baby, and Emily had a Winslow Homer. The Cassatt is small-scale rendition of a painting in the museum in Richmond. It's nicely done, but you don't get a Cassatt for $50,000.00. The Winslow Homer is a seascape. It's a good painting, but not by Homer. I think I know who did it, but I need to look it up."

"How much did that set her back?"

"$65,000.00 or so," the Captain replied. "That is the cost of a frame for a Homer. American art gets top dollar. Ellen seemed to have paid $50,000.00 for the Cassatt. It's a French Impressionist by an American Artist. The mind boggles that someone could think they pick one up for under a half million. They are nice women, but not into art. Both thought the pictures were pretty and they vaguely knew the artist were famous.

"Emily liked the painting, but wasn't too sure about the cost. It could have been $75,000.00. She also said she thought it would have been bigger for the price. She expected it to be sofa-sized. I asked her if she had it insured. The nice man who sold it to her said the insurance was part of the price, so she didn't need to worry."

"Who was the nice man?"

"Poor Emily didn't remember," he said. "This has the makings of a perfect crime. Assuming the con men don't get caught right away, the witnesses would not be able to testify."

"There must be some financial records of the transactions," I said.

The Captain disagreed. "I was the executor of a cousin's estate. He had Alzheimer's and his records were either missing or undecipherable."

"Does anyone here help the residents with that sort of thing?"

"I don't know, but I think so," he answered. Glenn had seen us chatting and he joined us.

"Glenn, I was chatting with a friend and it seemed to me she was slipping. Is there someone here who could help her with her finances? She's getting very confused," the Captain asked.

"Officially Henry Paulus is in charge of all the transitional patients, and they offer some sort of a service, but I don't know who does it. It's not Henry," Glenn said. "Who are you worried about?"

"Emily Carlisle," Captain Green replied. "She was a dear friend of my wife."

"I'll check on her tomorrow," Glenn said. "I know she's been slipping."

At five o'clock then next morning, I got a call from the Captain. There had been a fire in Emily Carlisle's house. She was dead. I called Glenn and Larry and we were there by 6:30. Larry went to help Jon who was in a state, almost in shock. Glenn went to help some of the residents who took it badly. He seemed to be able to calm them down.

I went to the burned building. The firemen were finishing up and the Fire Marshall, Vince Desoto, had just arrived. He was a friend of mine. He saw me. I was wearing my Essex Park uniform.

"Hey, he yelled, "Are you a maintenance man?"

"Yes sir!"

"Come over here and give us some help," he ordered.

When I got over to him he whispered, "What in hell are you doing here?"

"Working on a case," I replied.

"Oh shit," he said. "Is this incident a part of the case?"

"It's a fraud and possible financial shenanigans case," I said. "Up until I got a call this morning I'd have said there was a one-in-a-million chance there would be violence. I was wrong."

"This woman was involved?"

"She was a possible victim," I said.

Glenn came over with a file. "I have Mrs. Carlisle's medical records and contacts," he said. "It has a list of all of her medications. There is nothing unexpected in the list."

"Do you know anything about the night guard, Elizabeth Smith?" DeSoto asked. "She seemed to be drunk and had passed out. The guard house reeked of gin."

"Lizzy doesn't drink," Glenn said. "She had a serious liver disease and can't take a drop. I'd test her for a sedative."

"Does she take sedatives?" DeSoto asked.

"No, she always has a pot of Navy style coffee, so strong it makes hair grow on your chest. I'd test the coffee too." Glenn said as he handed the file to DeSoto. Someone was calling for him, so he left us.

"I bet that boy would love it in the ass," DeSoto whispered to me. "Have you tried him out yet?"

"He is a member of the club," I said.

"Do you have first dibs?"

"First come, first served," I said, "I don't know if he bottoms." Vince just smiled. I thought I had good gaydar, but obviously, his was more finely tuned.

I hadn't seen the Captain yet, but he appeared out of the early morning gloom.

"Captain Green, this is Fire Marshall DeSoto," I said in introduction.

"This may sound odd, but I need to go in the house and look at something," Green said. "It's very important. I was in the house yesterday. I can tell if anything is amiss."

"He's with me," I whispered to Vince.

"We can all do a quick inspection," DeSoto said. The fire had been in the rear of the house, but the front rooms were smoke and water damaged. "We found her in the bedroom." We went in the house. Burned houses make me feel sick. My Aunt's body had been found in her burned house. The house looked defiled. This house smelled the same as my Aunt's.

"I need to look at the living room," the Captain said. "Get some light above the sofa." He was use to giving orders and the fireman obeyed.

There was a picture hanger there, but no painting. We looked at the sofa, on the floor and at the space behind the sofa. There was no sign of the Winslow Homer. I felt nauseated. This was the home of a nice, gentile lady. There was soot covered floral wallpaper on the walls, and the tables had porcelain curios mostly of flowers and birds. Brick-a-brack covered every surface. Everything was conventional and ordinary. It wasn't the home of a murder victim. For some reason she was killed and burned up.

"Have you seen what you wanted?" DeSoto asked. The Captain nodded. He looked pale and shocked.

"I personally think this is a tragic accident that requires only routine investigation," I said. "It may not be a fast investigation since other matters are more pressing."

"That will be my official report," DeSoto said. "I'll have something in a few months. Where can I talk with you privately?" he asked. "It may be a few hours from now."

"At my house," the Captain replied, "I'll be waiting." He gave DeSoto his address.

Billy Fillmore, my client arrived and talked with Vince. I made it a point not to talk with him, since I didn't want anyone to see me with the owner of the security company. I did hear him protesting about the sobriety of Liz Smith. As Billy left, he winked at me.

Later I heard a television report about a tragic fire and death at Essex Park. The reporter reminded older people to be careful with frayed electrical cords. That sounded good to me. When I went by Mrs. Carlisle's house, I saw Vince had the senior investigators of his department there along with a crime scene lab. This was the A team, not the second string.

Larry came by. He was going to each residence and checking the fire detectors. He was also telling them about a memorial service planned for the evening. Jon and Henry were working on it. That event would occupy all of the senior staff, so I was left alone and unobserved. I could get together with Vince and then Captain.

The Captain was fuming. He wanted to strangle someone, but he didn't know who. It told him DeSoto was top of the line.

"He's older than I am," he said. "I heard something about an electrical cord. That's shit."

"Vince has retired about five times and he keeps getting called back. He can smell arson better than a blood hound," I said. "Firehose is just as determined too."

"Firehose?"

"It's his nick name. Vince and I share a common physical characteristic."

"I could see you are the same height," the Captain said. Vince was six feet two or three. "I guess you know him real well?"

"Real well," I replied.

It was after 11:00 when DeSoto arrived at the Captain's house.

"What's this about a frayed electrical cord?" Green asked. "Emily was fastidious about that sort of thing."

"We just didn't mention it had been frayed with a knife," DeSoto answered. "We like to keep the perpetrators relaxed. That nurse was right. Someone tampered with the night guard's coffee. It was a prescription sedative, borderline overdose. She's a big woman. If she had been 50 pounds lighter, she'd be dead. Okay men, what's going on here? Tell me everything."

I outlined what we knew about the case. The Captain explained his role. He thought he had precipitated the death by discovering the fake Winslow Homer.

"It's unusual for a white collar crime to turn to violence," Vince said. "If this was a fraud perpetrated on Alzheimer's patients, it was calculated to avoid violence. The victims have self-erasing minds. You couldn't have anticipated this. Do you have anyone you suspect?"

"No. I think Henry Paulus is a snake, but I can't believe he would do anything physical," the Captain said. "I only see him here. He may have disreputable friends on the other side of our gatehouse."

"I'm working on that," I said. "He has another life in Richmond."

"Is the nurse okay?" Vince asked.

"Glenn? One hundred percent reliable," the Captain said. "When my wife was sick he was a godsend. I tried to give him some money to thank him and he refused. He had been through a rough patch in his life. Nursing my wife reminded him of why he became a nurse. That was enough. He knows his stuff too. Glenn keeps an eye on the problem residents and heads off problems before they get out of hand."

"He knows the Essex Park staff well too," I said. "He's a good judge of character."

"Captain Green if you could keep your ears open at the memorial service tonight, I'd appreciate it," Firehose asked. "Are you going, Clydesdale?"

"No. I'm new here; it would be too suspicious. I carpool with Glen and Larry, the young intern, so I'll be here late."

Maybe you could bring Glenn home with you tonight and I could talk with him?" DeSoto asked.

"It may be hard to do that without Larry guessing something is up," I said.

DeSoto laughed. "You can cross that boy off your list," he said. "His daddy is Paul Waldorf of Waldorf's department store. His momma is Elissa Battenburg, of the Battenburg & Sons Brokerage house. My grandsons know him. He's one of the few of their friends who isn't a spoiled brat. He's worth fifty or sixty million from his grandfathers trust fund."

"He didn't mention his last name," I said. "I've never heard of him."

"His full name is Paul Lawrence Wyeth Waldorf IV. They have more money than God, but they aren't into show. Larry can spend most of his life giving money away. Elissa is interested in care for the elderly," Firehose explained. "My guess is he's doing field work for her foundation."

The memorial service was at six thirty. I was glad I didn't go to it. It was broadcast on the closed circuit television system so I saw it in the locker room. I'd have had a hard time staying composed. Jon, to give him credit, did a good job. He was reassuring and comforting. He started by saying he wasn't going to talk about her death. He would only talk about her life and the love she brought to her friends and family. Henry read a bible verse and remarkably, I didn't get the dry heaves. The Captain gave an appreciation. It was short but appropriate.

After the service, I collected Larry and Glenn and we went to Richmond. I asked if they'd like a drink at my apartment. Both men said yes. It was about nine when we got to my place. It's above the headquarters of Clydesdale & Company, but there was only a small sign, neither Glenn or Larry noticed. A cold beer really hit the spot. We had all downed two beers by the time Firehose arrived fifteen minutes later. Then we had another round of beers.

We were all tired and needed to wind down. Firehose was coated in dirt and soot. I had been working since six and was tired and dirty. "I need a shower, Clydesdale," Firehose announced. "Have these boys seen your bathroom?"

"Not yet. They just got here," I said.

"We could all use a little freshening up," Larry said.

"Well the shower is big enough for all of us," Firehose said. We trooped off to my bedroom and the shower. My shower room-bath is an extravaganza of azure tiles with multicolored, bas-relief, ceramic parrots and palm trees. A decorator had miss ordered the tiles and the tile man installed it in his apartment above the store. It looked like a 1930s stage set and had room for six.

No one in our group was shy and as before, Larry was hard as soon as he saw big meat. This time Glenn was looking at Firehose and he was erect too. "Sorry about that," he said.

"It's nice to be appreciated," Firehose replied. Glenn got to Firehose before Larry did. I got to sample the boy's lavender cock head. It was all I hoped for. After a lick, the cock juices began to flow. I hadn't had the opportunity to suction the goo from his cock before. Some guys get hard easily, but it takes a real workout to get the juice. Sometimes you only get a brief taste before the cream spurts. Larry was a taste treat.

While I sucked Larry, Firehose and Glenn did some quick negotiating. Firehose liked to top, and Glenn wasn't sure he could take it. Firehose thought he could. "Let me make you a proposition," Vince said. "If I can get the first five or six inches in, I get to go the rest of the way. If the first half is too much, we'll call it a day."

To tell you the truth, I wasn't sure Firehose was sincere about that. I knew the length of his cock wasn't the problem. It was the diameter. Glenn agreed. He was no fool and knew the entire organ would end up in his ass one way or another.

I was amused by the conversion. Larry loved it. The pre cum flowed in a direct relationship with his state of arousal. He was turned on. I got the lubricant and some poppers out. Larry took the lead in opening Glenn's ass. He had learned well and got Glenn open and turned on. Larry's hands were slimmer and longer than Glenn's. He discovered Glenn's Magic nut right off the bat and he used it as a punching bag for his finger.

I helped lubricate the fire hose. Vince had no problem staying hard, but he liked the attention. Larry was on his hands and knees as he worked on Glenn's ass. Downy hair covered Larry's ass, with longer hairs at the puffy and slightly swollen hole. I took a little lubricant and coated Larry's hole. I thought a little salve would feel good since I had opened him up earlier. I wasn't going lubricate the sphincter or the tunnel. I figured Larry needed some rest.

Larry's ass all but dilated. He was in the mood and more than receptive. Soon, Larry and Glen were now on their knees, watching as they prepared to get fucked. I wouldn't say we exactly did synchronized fucking, but we came damn close. Larry's ass must have remembered the earlier experience and it opened for me.

Glenn was so excited watching me fuck Larry, Vince was beyond the halfway point before Glenn noticed how big it was. Once he was all the way in, Vince pulled out, flipped Glenn and fucked him again. I got Larry to 69 with Glenn. Larry's ass still looked needy and I popped in for a second time that night. This arrangement gave both of them a front row seat to watch the other being fucked. They knew what they were watching was all but identical to what was happening to their holes.

After five or ten minutes, Glenn said. "I need a rest." We all did. We broke apart and cooled down. Vince was on his back, with the fire hose sticking straight into the air. Before I knew what was going on, Larry straddled Vince and impaled himself on the older man's cock. The younger man did a pole dance on the erect cock and Vince began to shoot. Larry loved that.

I figured turn about was fair play, so as Larry lay on the floor panting, I sat on his cock. As the lavender knob rubbed my prostate, he began to shiver and shake. His ejaculations were strong enough to tickle my rectum. I bounced on the erect member and he gave my chute a cum bath. He was almost crying it felt so good. Glenn was on the floor next to Larry, so I sat on him next.

I looked him in the eye just before I sat on his meat. I think he was grateful. His cock was uncut and thick and it really hit the spot as it slid in to my rectum. With Larry's cum lubricating the way, it felt great. Glen rolled me over and fucked me like a dog in heat for about ten minutes when he and I both shot off.

Part 5

The next morning I was with the crew cleaning up the area around Emily Carlisle's house. Jon wanted to have as few reminders of the tragedy as possible. That made sense to me. That sort of thing wasn't supposed to happen in a place like Essex Park.

Emily didn't have children. A cousin in the Midwest was the closest relative. Jon contacted the cousin. She deeply distressed, but was going through chemotherapy for breast cancer and was in no condition to deal with the death. Her husband was a retired naval officer, and had met the Captain on a visit. After a flurry of phone calls and faxes, Captain Green was appointed co-executor and he was put in charge of the funeral arrangements and cleaning out the house.

Green told Jon he would appreciate it if he could get some help with the cleanup and heavy work. He asked for me. Jon agreed. I'd been in Richmond for years so I had funeral connections. Emily had been Episcopalian and Green was Presbyterian. I got in touch with Wally, an organist in the most upscale Episcopalian Church in town. He knew everyone and knew exactly who to call. I knew a funeral director and he took care of everything. The body was at the medical examiner's lab, but once it was released, everything was on automatic pilot. That made it easier for the Captain and Emily's friends.

Captain Green wanted to get to the bank statements as soon as possible. The banks weren't too willing to do that, but Fire Marshall DeSoto took care of that. The Captain and the Fire Marshall overpowered the branch manager. I got my accountant to help. Frank was a forensic accountant who had a nose for financial irregularity.

When the investigators finished, we got into the house. Cleaning up is good way to go over everything in detail. I started in the living room. The Captain worked on the library-den. He was looking for records. Vince called me on my cell phone. "We didn't find a purse, wallet, or checkbook," he said. "If you find them let me know."

I told the Captain about the call. "Curious, isn't it?" he said. I nodded. There was no way a seventy-year-old lady would be without a purse. As yet, we didn't have any of the final lab reports on Emily or Liz, the guard, but the potential for an accidental fire was diminishing at a breakneck pace.

As I cleaned up the living room, I found no trace of the Homer. I did find a well-framed Audubon bird print sitting behind an armchair. I guessed it preceded the Homer on the wall behind the sofa. It would have matched the decoration in the rest of the house. There was no trace of the suspect painting.

Looking out the soot-covered window, I saw an array of bird feeders and a birdbath. A card table sat near the window had an unfinished game of solitaire on it, and a *Bird's of Eastern North America* book. There were four chairs. I guessed she played Bridge. I couldn't guess what she known, or done to cause her death.

"I found last year's records," The Captain called from the next room, "They were in the secretary. Old check records are here too." I went to the library and looked at the checks. Emily had neat and orderly handwriting and each check was carefully recorded. If there were a checkbook in her purse, it would tell a tale. We didn't find it. I wondered if a woman might be involved. A woman would be more likely to remember the purse.

At this point most of the investigative work was going on in the State labs and in Richmond. I had people investigating Henry Paulus and the Miller galleries, as well as looking into Mrs. Carlisle's finances. The Captain and I were much engaged in funeral arrangements .The funeral was to be at 10:30 on Friday and there was a reception afterward at Essex Park. Mrs. Carlisle and her late husband weren't Virginia natives, so most of the people at the service were from Essex Park. The service was nicely handled, and it seemed to release tension. Funerals provide closure.

It wasn't closed for the Captain or me. He was a driven man. There was no way he would be happy until the murderer was in jail. We agreed on that. I didn't go to the funeral since I didn't know the woman and I wanted to remain in the background. I worked at the house, getting rid of any evidence of a fire on the outside.

A local nursery provided new plants to replace those damaged by the firemen. We got a few loads of sod to fix the lawn. It was a long day for me, but by five it looked great. I went by the Captain's to see how the funeral had gone. He said all had been perfect and he thanked me for my advice. "I'm sort of a bull in the china shop when it comes to funerals," he said. "My wife use to do that sort of thing. Your pals got it just right."

"Well, I said, "You had the best gay organist, caterer and florist in Richmond. If they can't get it right, they will get kicked out of the gay union. Sensitivity is the name of the game."

He laughed. "I guess you're right about that. I'm bushed."

"Me too. It's been a long week," I said.

There was a long silence. "I have something odd to ask you, " he said. "If you get offended, just forget I said anything."

"To tell you the truth, it takes a lot for me to get offended," I said. "Shoot."

"I'm going to visit a few friends on the Eastern Shore this weekend. They're all retired military and we all share the same interests," he said. "I mentioned to Karl, the host, I had met a really horse hung man. He asked if I could bring you along. I guess you could say it's a sex party. We're all older men."

"Am I the door prize?"

"You are offended!" the Captain exclaimed. He was worried.

"If there is a lot of sex, I'm usually game. I do like to top. Did you mention that?" I asked.

He smiled. "That's not going to be a problem. Karl wanted to know if you were a top." I agreed to go with him.

I went home with Glenn and Larry. They were relieved the funeral was over. They were on call that weekend and were hoping the residents would calm down. The next morning the Captain picked me up at nine and we drove to the eastern shore.

Virginia's Eastern Shore always struck me as an accident and a failure of the mapmakers' art. It is completely detached from the mass of Virginia by the Chesapeake Bay. It sits all by itself connected to the rest of the state by the modern bridge-tunnel. We got to Karl's place just before lunchtime. Karl lived in a handsome house in the middle of a large farm of several hundred acres. I would guess the house dated from around 1800 and it was in beautiful condition. Most of the property had grown up, so it was completely secluded from the road. It was a private as a house could be.

Karl was a retired Captain in the Navy. The only other guest was Col. Bull O'Brien, a Marine. Bull was mad. He had been forced to retire because of his sexual tenancies. Oddly, that was an excuse to cover the real reason they got rid of him. He was a Middle Eastern expert and was unhappy with the Pentagon's policy for the war in Iraq. As he watched the war turn into a disaster, he just got madder.

He was a body builder and exercise fanatic, and looked at me askance. I wasn't his type at all. Karl was a courteous man who had served as a protocol officer in the Pentagon. He made sure visiting dignitaries were greeted and treated appropriately for their rank and station. He had been an attaché in several embassies, including Moscow and Beijing. I assumed he was in military intelligence.

Two men arrived shortly after we got there. Tommy was a former Master Sergeant, and Calvin was Chief Petty Officer in the Navy. Calvin had the most spectacular Alabama accent I had ever heard. He blew his nose with an accent. Tommy was an Italian from the Bronx. They were friends, but you would have thought they needed a translator.

We had sandwiches for lunch and then went to the back yard. It overlooked a narrow inlet of the Chesapeake Bay. An overgrown boxwood hedge defined one side of the yard. Karl led us through a gap in the bushes and we came to a circular pool. A fountain sprayed water across the pool. Karl stripped naked and jumped in. The rest of us followed shortly. The water was warm, but very clear and refreshing. We played around a bit, then I got out and dried off in the sun.

When O'Brien got out, he did a double take when he saw my cock. I love size queens and Bull was showing twelve of the ten danger signs of being a size queen. He had started to take a space on the other side of the pool, but decided to relocate next to me. Karl had been next to him on the other side. "Nice, isn't it?" Karl said as he glanced toward my cock.

"I've got first dibs," Bull replied as he relocated next to me. I don't think he knew how well sound carries across water. I'm not the shyest man in the world and not at all shy about my body. It would have been hard to hide my cock even if we were wearing trunks any way.

Bull had a great body. He was massive and powerful, he had clipped his body hair that formed an even mat on his chest. His bush hadn't been clipped and his cock and balls were compact and almost hidden in the hair.

Karl was physically the opposite. He was tall and lean with a runner's physique. He was shaved hairless with a neat cube of hair at his pubes. A long white snake hung from the cube. His low hanging ball sack held the jewels. They were the size of ripe plums. He was cut and his cock head was the size of the balls.

The Captain, Calvin and Tommy joined us. Tommy was hairy and slightly built. Calvin was massive and smooth. We chatted for a while, but no one wanted to make the first move. When Karl was standing next to me, I took the opportunity to suck him. It was as if someone had shot off a starting gun.

Our sextet turned to three clusters of sucking men. After a few minutes we broke apart, relieved that the sex had started.

"You sure are a friendly group of men," I said. "Nice and welcoming,"

"You've got a lot to welcome," Bull said.

"I'm not a very refined guy," I added, "While I like to suck, I really like to top. Is that a problem?"

Karl, Bull and Tommy said, "This is your lucky day!" in unison. We all burst out laughing. Karl's dog started to bark so he went off to see what it was. I decided to see what Bull wanted. Actually, I knew what he wanted, but I didn't know what he could take.

Bull turned his attention to me, or, more correctly, to my cock. I may not have been his type, but my cock made up for my physical shortcomings. I must admit, Bull was neither shy nor inexperienced, but before we could get down to serious business, Karl returned with two more guests. One was a younger man in his thirties and the other was a man I remembered seeing on the television as a Pentagon consultant.

Everyone slowed down to greet the newcomers and to let them catch up. I will say they did that quickly. The young man was Rich, he had been an Arabic translator for the Army. The older man was simply called Hank. Both were new to the group. Rich was now living in Richmond, and while he was an Army man, he exemplified the Marine Gung-Ho attitude. He was a sexual spark plug and he got things going.

Rich was perhaps the most average man in the world. He was average in weight and height, average looking and had standard issue equipment too. You would never pick him out in a crowd. He loved sex and he wasn't at all shy about getting it.

Hank was distinguished looking but reserved, somewhat like Captain Green. Once he got going he was a sensual man. I think he may have been nearly 70 years old, but he had no problem maintaining an erection. He was uncut and hung. Hank wouldn't go looking for sex, but if it passed his way, he would take it. Once he had the ball, he would run with it.

As we talked, I heard thunder in the distance. It was hot and muggy, so we left the pool and went inside. I've been to my share of sex parties and usually sex is in a playroom. Here we split up and went to individual bedrooms. I ended up in a room with Bull and Rich. I could tell Bull and my cock excited Rich. Rather oddly, Rich instinctively seemed to know Bull wanted to be fucked and he set about getting Bull ready for the penetration. He offered to do a lubricating fuck to open Bull's ass.

"What in hell is a lubricating fuck?" Bull asked.

"Well, I coat my cock and your ass with as much lube as possible and then shove it in deep." Rich explained. "If you're planning to take that monster cock your bed-mate sports, deep lubrication is what you need. If you're open minded, I can shoot some of the home brewed lubricant really deep."

"You shoot a big load?" Bull asked as he stroked Rich's meat. Rich was playing with Bull's ass.

"When I'm turned on it can hit the ceiling," Rich said. "I'm just about as turned on as I've ever been in my life."

"Give me the full treatment," Bull said. I could tell Rich amused him. Rich coated his cock and eased it into Bull's ass. Bull was excited and took it easily. Rich's shaft was on the thin side, but the knob was big. That suited Bull just fine. Rich pulled out, squirted some lube into Bull's ass, and then used his cock to shove it deep.

Rich did this twice then made a dozen deep strokes in quick succession and shot off. He shook and shivered with each ejaculation. Bull loved that. When Rich pulled out, he was still drooling cum. I nosed my cock head into the quivering hole. Bull was on his back and I took his legs, spread them wide, and pushed them open. I wanted Bull to be defenseless. I played with his hole, pushing the head in part way but just stretching the sphincter, not popping it.

Bull had buns of steel, so he wasn't entirely defenseless. I knew he wanted my cock, but sometimes your body isn't so sure about a large object lodging itself in your ass. I also didn't know if Bull wanted my cock just because it was big, or because he liked to be fucked. Some guys are more into the achievement than the sensation.

I bounced and pressed my cock until Bull opened for me. I didn't pop through it, he wanted it so bad he just opened up. Usually I stop once I'm in to the let a guy get his bearings. This time I pushed in deep until my curly pubes tickled his ass. I didn't shove it in, I just pushed in a single slow movement. Bull's eyes crossed and he sighed. A second or two later, his sphincter tightened, trying to grab my cock and keep it in his ass.

Once I was in, he wanted it in. I jiggled my cock to see how we would react. It was all I could wish for. He could hardly breathe when I moved. I would pump a little and he would try to grab my cock with his violated sphincter. We had a nice, friendly battle until he unconditionally surrendered. By then my cock was freely traveling into the depths of his rectum and he was either moaning, begging me to stop or begging me to fuck him harder.

The other guys visited the room to watch. Some were amused; all were turned on. When Karl leaned over to whisper encouragement into Bull's ear, Hank popped his cock into Karl's ass effortlessly. On the other side of the Room, Calvin was bent over with Captain Green slow fucking him. Rich fucked Tommy, the hairy Italian.

I was having a great time until I went too far and shot everything I could into Bull's ass. I bellowed, "I'm shooting!" as I climaxed. This seemed to precipitate a general round of orgasms. When I pulled out, I got on the bed, straddled Bull's cock and sat on it. I don't think more than half of his organ was in my ass before he popped. His whole body shivered and bucked as he popped. I wasn't big enough to hold him down, so I had to ride the bucking bronco. He got deep. When he calmed down, I played with his tits and he stroked the hair on my chest.

He was still having aftershocks, and I remained turned on. He was still hard and I did a little hula dance on his pole. His knob made the perfect connection with my prostate and I lobbed a couple of volleys over his chest. Bull opened his mouth the catch the last shot. As he swallowed it, I felt his cock twitch.

The room was quiet with everyone recovering. There must have been a general exchange of cum. I had a friend who said the orgasm wasn't over until the last drops drooled from the slit. I got off Bull's cock and was next to him. "I've never tasted another man's cum before," he said.

"Are you okay with it?" I asked.

"I think I could get use to it," he replied.

"There are drinks in the other room," Kurt announced. There had been a small thunderstorm as we played in the bedroom, but the sun was shining again. The room remained hot, but the humidity had abated, we left the bedroom and walked naked back to the pool. The men were relaxed now and any initial shyness or reserve was gone.

The change was most noticeable in the Captain and Hank. Their trips up Karl and Calvin's backsides had broken through their natural reserve. The Captain came over to me, "Was that as good as it looked?" he asked. I said yes.

"I had no idea Bull was available," he added, "I thought he was a pure top."

"He may be, all top. Sometimes guys get inspired some times to try out new things," I said, "But I know he ain't pure no more!" I fondled the Captain's cock. He was still dripping a little, so I tasted it.

He watched me do this and simply said, "Damn!" I left me and walked over to Bull who was lying on a towel next to the pool. A little later, the Captain was fingering Bull's ass. He had relaxed.

I sat next to Rich and Tommy. "I had figured you for a bottom," I said to Rich.

"You figured right," he said, smiling, "but you could have figured me as bottom, a sideways, or a middle. Some guys are ambidextrous; I'm ambi-sexual. If you can do it with a cock, I like it."

"And boy, does he like it," Tommy said. We talked for a while as we recharged our balls. Investigation is usually 90% hard work and 10% good luck. I was lucky today. Rick had an apartment above an art gallery in Richmond, none other than the Miller Galleries of Americana. He knew the manager of the Gallery, R. Winston Jones, and he did part-time work for them translating letters and bills from Asian suppliers.

Rick was an expert in oriental languages, Hindi and Chinese as well as Arabic. Actually, Hindi and Chinese were his strong suit. His stepfather had been a Jordanian Engineer, and he had picked that up from him. I've never understood how a person could pick up a language, but that was what Rick could do.

"The funny thing is that the Americana in the Miller Galleries of Americana is mostly Chinese," Rick said. "There's a studio somewhere in Shanghai had produces Wild West pictures for them."

"That's America for you," Tommy said. "I'll bet there's a made in China mark on the inside of the Liberty Bell."

"The paintings cost a lot, most are a $1,000.00 to $1,500.00 at the current exchange rate," Rick explained. "Good old R. Winston has some art students who antique them and they even have an oven sort of thing that makes them look older."

"What do the sell them for?" I asked.

"That's funny," Rich said. "Nothing had a price tag on it. Everything is sold, "By Appointment only." The gallery is never open to the public. I don't know anything about art, other that I almost bought a sofa sized painting from the back of a truck in a K-Mart parking lot once. R. Winston told me they never advertise. People know them by word of mouth only."

"R. Winston must be quite a character," I said.

"That he is," Rich said. "He has an English accent he got from going to the movies. I think Hugh Grant is his model. As far as I can tell, he's from Michigan. That's the accent under the accent."

"Is he good in bed?" I asked.

"I never kiss and tell," Rich said. I looked at him with disbelief. He burst out laughing. "To tell you the truth I'm way too old for him. He has a pal, a guy named Henry, and they seem to import Asian boys for their mutual enjoyment. I've met a few of them. Henry and R. Winston think they are getting genuine teen-age chicken. Most of the "boys" are in their 20s, but one or two were 30. They looked young."

"I'm not into teenage sex," Tommy said.

"Nor am I, Rich said. "I like my beef aged. I talked with several of the "boys." Life is rough being gay in China. Pretending to be a 14-year-old and being fucked by two American Queens seemed like a good deal to them. Once and a while they get poked by some of R. Winston's clients, but the guys seemed to like that.

Part 6

The Captain and Bull joined in our conversation. Bull said he had a friend who had just gotten a new houseboy-playmate. "From what I could gather, you could get the house boy permanently, or for a weekend," Bull explained, "To put it mildly, I'm not into boys, or men who pretend to be boys, so I didn't get any details."

"Is the pimp named Henry?" I asked.

"I don't know about that, but my friend mentioned the boy came from Richmond," Bull said. "It apparently is very private and exclusive."

"Where did your friend live?" I asked.

"In northern Virginia," Bull answered. "If you were hiring playmates, it would be good to use a Richmond supplier. They are sensitive to foreign sex slaves in D.C."

"Did your friend by any chance just buy a painting?" the Captain asked.

"How in hell did you know that?" Bull exclaimed. "The conversation started when he told me he had bought a good painting at a bargain price. My friend is wealthy, but not as loaded as he's like to be. You know, three or four million."

"Did he say who the painter was?" I asked.

"I'm not into art much," Bull confessed. "It was some Italian name like Pissa, maybe Pizzeria."

"Pissarro?" the Captain suggested.

"That's it," Bull said. "You're really up on this sort of stuff."

"Purely a stab in the dark I assure you," the Captain said. "My wife was into that sort of thing. Pissarro is a French Impressionist."

"Sounds Italian to me," Bull said.

"What's wrong with being Italian?" Tommy asked.

"Is Pissarro a big time painter?" I asked.

"I would say he was either one of the lesser first string painters, or the top of the second string," the Captain replied

"We're not talking about a painter whose paintings go for a bargain price?"

"Not at all," he said. "It's hard to think anything short of a million would get a painting. Maybe a drawing or sketch would go for less. I'm interested in American nautical paintings. I have to satisfy myself with good works by lesser-known painters and with primitives. My wife gave me a fine painting when I retired from the Navy. It set her back $70,000.00 and it took a lot of doing to find it. She had good connections in the art world and many friends. One of them saw it in an out-of-the-way gallery and gave her a call. No one comes by your house and says, "By the way, I've got a bargain Pissarro you might like."

"You'd find them in a big New York or London auction house?"

"That's right," he said. "You'd be bidding against the Met and Japanese, or Arab billionaires. If you couldn't get a Renoir, or Monet, you'd be really happy with a Pissarro."

"Or a Cassatt, Remington, or Winslow Homer?"

"Actually, American paintings are very hot now," the Captain said. "There are no bargains in the top tier of painters. You'd have to be crazy to think you could get a bargain."

"That's the scam, isn't it?" I observed. "You find a retirement community for the rich, then you wait for age and dementia to take its toll."

"It's a vile scheme," the Captain said in disgust. "Vile."

"And we have the prostitution enterprise too," I said, "It seemed as if Henry is involved in a handful of suspect enterprises. I think he may trade in underage boys."

"Boys aren't my thing," the Captain said.

"Not mine either," I said. "I like my men full grown with some mileage. I hate breaking in a new model."

Tommy laughed. "Well if you like high mileage vehicles, you have hit the jackpot today."

"You mean you're not a virgin?" I asked.

He laughed, "Well you could say my warranties expired. Don't worry, though, I've replaced the spark plugs."

I wondered if the party was winding down, but then discovered it had just started. The Captain had failed to tell me it was a sleep over. Several men arrived in a Mercedes. They were retired Navy from Norfolk. Jimbo was a tall and impressive 65-year-old man. His friend was Roger. They made a Mutt and Jeff like pair. Jimbo towered over Roger.

Both got naked in record time and joined into the festivities immediately. Jimbo was a cum-hound. He loved man cream and sucking it from a cock. Roger was into asses. He topped. His cock was thin, longish and always hard. He tended to shove his cock into any available ass. Oddly, no one seemed to mind. He had an easy cock to take, and he was a rather jolly old man.

Jimbo almost magically appeared wherever there was cum. He preferred it fresh from the balls, but he didn't mind licking up the remains from your gut and chest. It may sound stupid, but his efforts kept things neat. Dried cum is hard to get off if you're hairy, and most of us were. Karl fixed a good dinner for us, and afterward I drifted off to the bedroom to see what was up.

No one was in the bedroom, so I got on the bed and planned to have a little post dinner nap. I might have dozed off for a little, but the Captain showed up. He got on the bed, beside me and reached over to play with my meat.

"Do you mind?" he asked.

"Shit no," I replied. "It's pretty rare when I'm not hot to trot."

"I've always been a man of action, but that didn't extend to sexual matters," he said. "It's hard for me to let my hair down, but I've been comfortable with you. You don't have many hang-ups, do you?"

"You noticed?"

The Captain smiled. "I was shocked seeing you with Bull. I've known Bull for 25 years. He makes Bruce Willis and Conan the Barbarian look like girly men. I've never seen him let his guard down until you were up his ass. He's always been in control before."

"Have you ever admitted you like sex to yourself?" I asked. "Has it always been a guilty secret?"

"I loved my wife, but sex was just a part of that experience," he said. "For pure physical pleasure and excitement, Glenn was a revelation. What I think Bull was feeling is still well beyond my comprehension."

"Give it time," I said. "I saw a book titled something like *My Best Orgasm*. A majority of the men in the book said it was their first experience. They all must have been doing it wrong. It gets better the more you do it. You like men and you like sex with men. Admit that to yourself and see what happens. Bull and Tommy came in the bedroom. Nature took its course.

On Monday, Fire Marshall DeSoto got the results back from the labs. Liz, the guard, and Mrs. Carlisle had both been drugged. Mrs. Carlisle had actually died from the overdose, not the fire. It's odd, but I felt better about that. To burn a person to death has always seemed to be more than murder to me. Liz had been perilously close to an over dose. There was one very interesting finding in the report. The drug used to put them to sleep wasn't pure. It had been adulterated.

"What does that mean?" I asked DeSoto.

"Adulterated drugs are rare in the US and Europe. Actually they are rare in the developed world in general. They're not that rare in Asia," he explained.

"Any chance they are homemade?" I asked. "Like crystal meth labs?"

"Nope, this drug requires sophisticated, expensive equipment and materials," DeSoto said. "It's not a lab in the basement sort of thing."

"Is China the best bet?"

DeSoto nodded.

"Shit, it's hopeless to trace then," I said.

"It's not quite hopeless," he replied. "The Chinese government isn't happy about the adulterated drugs. It badly hurts their exports. We've turned over the lab reports to their Embassy. They will see what they can do. They admit is an outside chance, but if they do find it there may be a firing squad in the future for the bad guys. The Chinese aren't prone to be forgiving."

After the conversation with DeSoto, I called Elliot and Sedgwick and told them about my conversation with Rich. They were more than interested. All of their bloodhound like tenancies were excited.

I then met with Gus who was investigating the Miller Galleries of Americana for me and told him about the Chinese "Old Masters." He asked if he could see the Essex Park Cassatt and the Remington. I called the Captain to see what he could do. He called me back and said perhaps Gus could be his nephew and visit for a while. He was planning a little memorial for Emily would be nice and he could visit residents for donations. " A memorial garden would be nice, I think," he said. "Can this Gus person be a Landscape Architect by any chance? Bill Davis, our grounds man is a friend. He can help provide cover."

"By the time he arrives at your house he will be," I replied.

Gus was game. "My Mom is into roses," he said. "I've spent hours working with her and what seems like years listening to conversations on roses. If your Captain wants a rose garden, I'm your man."

The Captain was nothing if not organized. He went to see Jon about the possible garden. Jon liked the idea. The residents had been spooked by Emily's death and he wanted to channel that energy into something constructive. He asked Larry and Bill Davis to work with him. He wasn't too sure about a landscape architect, but those worries vanished when he found out the Captain would pay for it.

The Captain got a hint that Jon was on the outs with Henry. While outwardly Henry had been shocked by the death, Jon had overheard him joking about "frying the bitch" and a "barbecued biddy." Henry had been talking with Tiffany Lewis and she found these comments amusing. Jon was disturbed. "Jon is clueless, but not bad," the Captain concluded

Two days later Gus arrived and met the Captain and Bill. The trio hit it off at first sight. Gus had a sketch for a small rose garden, labeled "A Garden to Celebrate the Life of Emily Carlisle." It was pretty and well thought out. Gus' mother provided the names of low maintenance roses, and even put a thorn less rose, the Zephirine Drouhin, at the entrances. It was very convincing.

"This looks real," I said.

"It is," Gus replied. "It's safer to have something real than to rely on bullshit." Gus and the Captain went off to visit residents to see if they might be interested in donating to the memorial. The day was a success.

There was golf tournament at Essex Park that day. Glenn and Larry had to stay until after the awards banquet, so I had to stay late. I went to the Captain's house at five. They had visited ten houses. They saw the Cassatt and found one other suspect painting. John Dell, an 88-year-old former stockbroker, had a Ned Wyeth in his entry hall.

"The paintings are cleverly done," Gus said. "The colors are right and the subject matter is perfect. The brush strokes are off, but a layperson wouldn't notice that. I think they cut and pasted some figures from Wyeth illustrations and then used that as the basis for the new Wyeth. There was one major error; the painting was too small. Wyeth's paintings were oversized. John thought it was an unused illustration from Treasure Island. By the way, I think they may have used old canvas."

"Old Canvas?"

"You find it in back rooms of shops and tucked away in attics," Gus said. "The paintings were just dirty enough to back up the story. The Wyeth had a label for the Brandywine Book Store, established 1897 in the frame. I think it was real. John told us a story of finding it in an attic in Wilmington."

"How much did he pay for it?"

"$15,000.00," the Captain said, "John whispered to me it had a little problem with provenance. It was found in the attic of a house that was being demolished, so it might not be 100% legal. It's a good line of bull."

Gus and the Captain were polite when they met in the morning. By five, they were an Uncle and his favorite nephew. I could tell they hit it off well. Once and a while there was a glint in the Captain's eye indicating more was involved. Gus wasn't particularly tall, but he was brawny. As a sculptor in stone, he had to be muscular. He was wearing a dress shirt and a tie, but they didn't hide the body beneath. He had huge, hairy hands and with his Greek coloring, he would be a good Ajax or Achilles.

I knew little about his personal life, but recalled he had been partnered and had died recently. I had been away on assignment when it happened and by the time I got back it was old news. Gus wasn't a full-time employee of Clydesdale & Company. We called him when we needed his skills. I knew Gus was gay, but I had no personal experience with him.

Bill Davis and Glenn came over at six for dinner. The Captain was a good cook, but it turned out Gus was a great cook. Apparently, his father had owned a restaurant, he could slice, and dice like a madman. We made a cheerful and compatible group. The mutual sexual attraction did nothing to reduce the good mood. The wine didn't hurt either. The banquet was over at 8:30 and we were really happy by then. Larry came by and joined us for after dinner drinks.

Larry sat at table next to Henry and Tiffany. They were with several older ladies, most of whom were deaf or partially deaf. As was their wont, they were all sweetness and kindness until the ladies left the table when they reverted to type. "It was a real Dr. Jekyll and Mr. Hyde situation," Larry said. "They had a few cocktails before and wine with dinner and they assumed most of the room was deaf."

"They were right about that," Glenn said. "They didn't notice you?"

"I'm an intern," Larry said. "I don't count in their book. I think the booze made them indiscreet. They had an extended joke about old cows that needed to be milked. Henry said he'd do the cows; Tiffany could milk the bulls. Tiffany laughed at that and said Henry had more practice at milking bulls than she did. Then they went into a discussion of sale prospects."

"Did you overhear that part?" I asked.

"I got a few names," Larry said. He paused. "Can you tell what's going on? I thought there was something odd going on here. To me it sounds like a scam is a foot. A friend of mine who works at the State Lab told me to watch my ass. That only could mean there is something's wrong with Mrs. Carlisle's death."

I told him and the rest of the group the full story. There was a slight chance Glen or Bill was involved, but the cat was already out of the bag. I didn't need to worry. Bill had seen the car from the art gallery at several other houses and had wondered what was up. The Captain took notes of the names and said he would visit them the next day. We combined the houses Bill had noted with the persons mentioned by Henry and Tiffany. I asked Glenn if these persons were suffering from early forms of dementia.

He told us he couldn't ethically reveal medical records. "I could tell you if a resident is healthy I guess," Glenn offered. "You might be able to jump to a conclusion if you want from that information."

That worked for us. An hour or so later we had a list of seven residents we hadn't known about. It was late and the Captain was a good host. We went through a lot of booze. I wasn't flat out drunk, but I was borderline.

"I'm afraid none of you boys are in any condition to drive home. I think you should stay here," the Captain announced. "I've got an extra bedroom and there's a couch in the den, if you don't mind sharing." It was late and no one was opposed spending the night. After some confusion, the Captain and Gus took the bed in the guest room. The rest of us shared the king sized bed in the master bedroom. Actually, Bill was going to sleep on a couch, until we all shared a shower.

Over the years, I've spent many hours in showers. I like being naked and a shower gives you an acceptable reason to be nude. I like sex too. I know there are men who are into man smells and sometimes into stench. I'm not one of them. Good sex can be messy anyway, so I like it when you start with a clean slate. With my uncut cock, I can be ripe by the end of the day, but I try not to be beyond the sell by date. I love the musky smell of cocks. The rich brew of precum, hormones with a dash of sperm if good for me. It's even good if it's been stewed in the foreskin. The shower gets everything off to a good start.

We didn't start sharing the shower. I stripped to take a shower and Larry asked if I would like some company. I said sure. Glenn and Bill came in the room and saw us. Larry is young. When he dropped his pants, he was at half-staff. I was feeling a bit randy too, and I had firmed up. Glenn took this in stride, but Bill's jaw dropped. He looked like a six year old who just saw what Santa had left under the tree.

"We're going to take a shower," Larry said.

"Is there any extra room?" Glenn asked.

"I don't know. It may be a little snug, but we can work something out, I'm sure," Larry answered. He put his arm around my shoulders and stroked his cock with his other hand. As I said before, Larry wasn't shy.

Bill glanced at Glenn who was already half naked. I didn't know a man could strip as quickly as Bill.

Bill was handsome in a Marlboro man way. His equipment was average, but the whole package was a knock out. Bill was torn between looking at Larry, who also was handsome, and at my cock. We wedged ourselves in the shower and all got wet and soapy.

It was tight, but just right. There was a little room to move, but you couldn't move without genital contact. In some situations like this, guys pretend they don't notice everyone was hard. This wasn't one of those occasions. Larry got on his knees and sucked the three of us. I was in the middle. Bill and Glenn had their arms around me and we were kissing. Our cock heads were touching, so Larry could lick the precum drooling from our slits with one swipe of his tongue. He gripped Bill and Glenn's balls, so he could pull them closer if they strayed.

When Larry came up for air, Bill dropped to his knees and started sucking. Bill wanted to inhale our cocks and balls. Glenn was in the middle now, so Bill grasped my ball sack with his left hand and Larry's with his right. Larry was interested in precum, so he concentrated on the cock heads in general and the slits in particular. Bill liked the shafts too as well as the balls. He treated Larry and my cocks like a harmonica. I don't know what tune he was playing, but it was good.

I took Bill's place next. Since I am short, I concentrated on the tender underside of the cock heads. I also decided to up the ante a little. I grabbed Bill and Glenn's balls to steady myself, but then decided I would hook a finger in their asses and hunt for their prostates. I guessed Glenn would be fine with this. I had no idea if Bill would like it.

I concentrated on Glenn's knob as I slipped a finger toward his hole. He jumped a little then relaxed. After playing with the hole for a second or two, I popped a finger through the sphincter, Glenn jumped a little then oozed a big glob of precum. Glenn was fine. I turned my attention to Bill's organ. He was drooling 100% Marlboro Man cock juice. He was making out with Glenn and Larry and was greatly excited. His ass hole twitched when I touched it and he moaned. His sphincter caressed my finger when it made contact. I got a second finger at his hole and then worked both into his ass hunting for his prostate.

I worked a second finger into Glenn's ass, then added a third to Bill's hole. Some people have one-tracked minds; others can multi-task. I am the later. With my left hand up Glenn's ass and my right hand up Bill's, I was still able to suck the three cocks and enjoy the banquet of ball juices. I found their prostates easily enough and gave them a finger massage.

"Hey, we're getting too close," Larry said. "Let's get on the bed and have some real sex." Everyone was ready. We were rolling around on the bed when the Captain dropped in.

"I thought you might need this," he said as he dropped off two tubes of lubricant and a bottle of Jungle Juice.

"Did you save some for yourself?" I asked. He just smiled and went to the guest room and to Gus. I later found out the Captain's ass was no longer virgin the next morning, and that Gus was fucked for the first time since his partner had died. It was a good night for both.

Larry's cock found a home away from home up Glenn's ass. Glenn was tight, but willing and it took a while, but was worth the effort. Technically, you could say I fucked Bill, but that wouldn't be correct. My cock occupied his ass and I gently massaged his rectum with it. He was tight, but I stretched him wide open; there was no real resistance. As I slowly pumped, his ass lining got sensitive. He got more responsive. I barely needed to move and he'd shiver. If I did a deep stroke, he would moan and gasp for air.

On one of the deep strokes, he shot off and promptly fell asleep. Larry was deep fucking Glenn pile-driver style. Glenn popped and crashed. Larry and I were alone with two sleeping men. We were back to back in the middle of the bed. Larry rolled over and eased his well-lubricated cock into my ass He put his arm around me and we fell asleep.

Part 7

The Captain and Gus went visiting the next day. I was working near the administrative offices. Jon was away for a day or two and Henry was in charge. Henry liked to throw his weight around and give orders. I noticed he liked doing this as a pure demonstration of power, not to achieve any positive objectives. He would get me to move a bush two feet so it would be "perfect." He did the same thing to the cooks in the kitchen and made Larry re-write some reports because he didn't like the indentation of the paragraphs.

All in all, Henry had the characteristics of a petty dictator. Tiffany was his accomplice, but I wasn't too sure she was a loyal follower. When Henry wasn't looking, she had an odd look on her face. It wasn't a look of pure hate I saw after she had talked to one of the old ladies. I think Tiffany saw Henry as a rung on a ladder. He was someone she would step on as she made her way up. I was lucky enough to be weeding a flowerbed next to the offices when Henry met with the Art Gallery owner, R. Winston Jones.

R. Winston struck me as a grade B actor playing the role of an art gallery owner. Perfectly groomed, he had a small mustache and every hair in place. He wore a tweed jacket with an Ascot. He was effeminate enough to be arty, but not offensively so. R. Winston was also a big, imposing man, maybe 6'-3" and 250 pounds. My guess was that not one of those pounds was muscle, but I wasn't sure about that.

"These paintings aren't cheap," R. Winston complained. "The originals cost two or three thousand, and the restoration adds another thousand or two. Can we up the price?"

"I guess we could up them a little, but there is a limit before the heirs' notice," Henry said. "We can't make any waves, only ripples. I'm not sure anyone here has enough marbles left to notice the new paintings, but if there are too many, someone might catch on."

"What about that woman who . . ." R. Winston began to ask.

"Not a word about that," Henry interrupted. "Not even to your closest and dearest."

"Any need for house boys here?"

"There's always a need for boy toys, but not here," Henry said. "How did Kim work out?"

"All that I could wish. He's a jewel," R. Winston said while chuckling. They went back to the offices and I returned to weeding. I discovered the area next to the side door of the offices was a favorite place for private cell phone conversations. I decided to re mulch the bed next to it and get it back to tip-top shape. I thought I might pick up on then office scuttlebutt.

I learned a lot about the personal problems of the cook and several of the maids. They all saw me working on the bed, but a gardener is just a gardener. I struck gold when Tiffany came out for a call. She kept her voice low at first, but as the conversation continued she got louder.

Fortunately, she also got louder when she was annoyed. That was for a good part of the conversation.

She talked about "that fucking fag." At first I couldn't tell if she was referring to Jon, or Henry. It later became clear the fucking referred to the man's favorite activity. John didn't fuck, so Henry was the object of her contempt. She was pissed at his "sideline." It might get them in trouble. "There's big jail time for that," she said. Later I heard the word "minors."

I couldn't hear the name of the person she was talking with. She referred to him or her as "dear" or "honey," but I wasn't sure if the person was a man or a woman. Whoever it was, I got the impression she was giving a report to a superior.

As soon as she went in the offices again I called my office and told them to do an in depth report on Tiffany and her associates. Around three, a pair of men came out of the offices. One was a high-powered executive type. The other man was a flunky of some sort. My nose told me the flunky was actually a bodyguard. I know the look and even a suit and tie can't hide it.

"I'll be in meetings for two or three hours," he told his flunky. "Wander around and check things out." The executive type went into the offices leaving the bodyguard outside.

The flunky walked over to me. "The flowers look good," he said. "Mr. Williams likes things neat."

"I do too. Will's the name," I said as I stood. I was all hot and sweaty again and my pants were a little tight.

"Mitch here," he replied. Mitch was one of those guys who checks out a guy's basket before he looks at the face. When he finally got to my face, I winked at him. He smiled. He realized he had gazed at my equipment too long, but I wasn't offended.

"I'm finished here," I said. "It's off to a house we're getting ready for re sale."

"Empty?" he asked. "Maybe I should look it over, just to make sure it's ready." I nodded and we went off to 47 Essex Park Crescent. Mitch wasn't the brightest bulb in the hardware store, but he knew what he wanted.

The residents of 47 had moved from the assisted living to the total care section of Essex Park. It had stayed empty for six, or seven months while the former residents dreamed they might get back into it. They finally decided to sell it. Both had been smokers and the unit needed a complete repaint and redecorating job. The painters were done, but the floor refinishing was next week. The key to the unit was at the back door.

Mitch was young, maybe 22 or 25, and he wasn't an actor. He unconvincingly asked me questions about the condition of the house we walked around the house. The minute we got inside, he had one interest, my cock. We looked around the house and went straight to the master suite bathroom. This had been totally renovated in pink marble focusing on a Jacuzzi.

"Does it work?" Mitch asked.

I turned it on. "Want to give it a spin?" I asked.

"Sure, if you want to," he said. I stripped off my shirt. Mitch took off his tie, and then his shirt.

"Damn, usually I'm the hairiest man in the room," I said. "You're a caveman."

"Sorry about that," Mitch said.

"I like a man who looks like a man," I said. "No one's going to mistake you for a girly man. You're a body builder?"

"I go to the gym," he answered.

"It shows," I said. He had a barrel chest, above a perfect six-pack. Mitch was burly so he didn't have the figure for a physique contest. He was more like a circus strong man. Curly, black hair covered every inch of his body. "Are you Italian?" I asked as we got in the whirlpool.

"Mom is Italian; Dad was Armenian," he replied. "I got a double dose of the hairy gene." We were both naked now. I stoked the hair on his chest and tweaked his tits. He moaned. Mitch fondled my equipment.

I was about half his size except in the cock and balls. He had beer can type cock, except it tapered as it vanished into his thick bush. It was almost a butt plug. I didn't know what Mitch liked. It turned out Mitch was 100 % a size queen and his only desire was to worship my cock. He loved it. At first, he just looked at it. He moved on to licking, and then to sucking. He wanted to take it all, but it wouldn't fit.

I licked him a little. Mitch rewarded me with a mouth full of cum. He had a full load of man cream in his balls. I had to swallow twice.

"Damn, I don't believe I did that," he said. "I wanted it to last longer. I'm no good once I've shot."

"What's your recharge time?" I asked.

"Fifteen, twenty minutes," he replied.

"It's the end of the day. I've got some time," I said. "How about you?"

Mitch smiled and then his attention wandered back to my cock. We talked. Fortunately, he was distracted. I was still stroking my meat and I coaxed some precum from my balls. A bead appeared on the slit and dripped into the water. Mitch loved that.

"I hope you don't get in trouble with Mr. Williams," I said.

"My Uncle is okay," Mitch said. "To tell you the truth, he's always happy when I'm out of the way. When Dad died, Mom got him to hire me to help financially. He doesn't like me much. I'm too much like Dad. They didn't get along well."

"Why is that?"

"He thought my Uncle played his business too close to the wrong side of the law," Mitch said. "It was a family business. It's better now than it used to be, but Dad didn't like it."

"A family business?" I asked.

He nodded. "My Uncle says everything is legit now." Mitch said. "He owns a series of retirement communities. They're all top of the line. No funny business at all. Mom even says so."

"Why is your Uncle here?"

"He doesn't like it when things happen," Mitch said. "He heard there were questions about that woman who died. Uncle Joe doesn't like that sort of thing. He doesn't like it at all."

As Mitch's balls recharged, his interest in my cock increased. I rotated back to the 69 position so he could take more of my cock. He was uncut. His cock was firm, but not hard yet. I worked my tongue into his pucker. Normally I like my cock juices fresh. Inside his foreskin was a rich stew of slightly fermented cum and precum. It didn't taste as good as the fresh stuff, but for some reason my cock got rock hard.

I knew Mitch wouldn't be able to deep throat my cock, but I figured his ass might be able to stretch enough. I fingered his hole. He jumped a little, but he also oozed a big glob of precum. I played with his hole. Soon he flooded my mouth with his man seed again.

"I'm going to have to get back," he said.

"How long are you going to be around here?" I asked.

"Until tomorrow night," Mitch said.

"Maybe we can work something out tomorrow," I suggested. He was interested. He went back to the office area.

Back in Richmond, I called Jonathan Lewis, one of my younger operatives. He was 27 years old, but looked as if he were 18. I asked him to make a visit to R. Winston's gallery. "Do you think you can be a young and eager intern?" I asked.

"All my roommates in college were art majors," he said. "I can talk the talk if I need to, unless it gets too technical."

"There is a chance being young and cute would be enough," I said.

"Should I play it swishy?" Jonathan asked.

"Young and vulnerable would be my guess," I said. "If he got the impression you're looking for a sugar daddy that might just hit the spot. I think R. Winston maybe running an upscale prostitution racket. He's into boys. He seems to be a forger too."

"Damn it, Clydesdale. You seem to run in some odd social circles," Jonathan remarked.

Gus called me later that night. He was staying with the Captain for another day. "We found a Constable in one house and a Georges Seurat. One house had a genuine Gilbert Stuart. It was a family portrait," he said. "The Constable was a good copy, but the Seurat was off, way off. Bad brushwork, and the forger used acrylic paint."

"The French Impressionists didn't use acrylic paints?"

"They weren't developed for 75 years after the impressionists," Gus explained. "My guess is the painter was making copy, but didn't know it was to pass as a forgery." I told Gus about the conversation I overheard between Henry and R. Winston.

"The copies were setting them back for $4,000.00 and $5,000.00. According to the people I talked with, they paid between $15,000.00 and $75,000.00. That's one hell of a markup," Gus said. "He wanted more?"

"It sounded that way to me. Con artists don't have a tradition of modest financial expectations," I said. "Over reaching can be their downfall. One thing bothers me. There is a con game, but I don't think Henry, or R. Winston had any idea anyone knew there was suspicions about the paintings. Why was Mrs. Carlisle killed?"

"Could she have had a moment of lucidity?" Gus asked. "Would she have known? Was she educated?"

"I'd ask the Captain about that." I said. "He might know."

Jon was back at work the next morning. He was meeting with Mr. Williams. I spent the day working on the golf course. It was pretty on the course, but there was no interesting conversation. I was surprised when Mitch and Mr. Williams came out to see me.

"Joe Williams," he said in introduction. He shook hands. "Unless I've I'm very mistaken, you're a guy called Clydesdale?"

"He's my twin brother," I said. Williams smiled.

"Sure, I believe you," he replied. "Let me level with you. I think something is wrong here. I'm not sure what, but there's something going on. The Home Atlantic Corporation owns Essex Park. HAC develops high quality housing for wealthy families. Thirty or forty years ago, some members of my family were rumored to have underworld connections. That's ancient history now. No rumors have ever been connected with HAC."

"I'm not interested in ancient history," I said. "I suspect the Statute of Limitations had resolved most of the problems any way. I am interested in what's going on here now."

"If any rumors pop up now, it could ruin the corporation." Williams said. "We've been over the books frontwards and backwards. We can't find anything. I can't believe Jon is involved. He did mention a problem with several staff members."

"Henry and Tiffany?"

"Oh shit. You know? Jon said they had attitude problems."

"It's a lot more than attitude," I said.

"Working their way into wills?" Williams asked.

"More subtle than that," I said, "but it's a con all right."

"Their fired!" he exploded.

"I'd rather keep them unaware they are under suspicion," I said, "As far as I can tell, they have no idea anyone knows." I explained the outline of the scheme.

"Penny ante stuff," he said contemptuously, "but what about the murder? Con men don't do that."

"There is the problem," I admitted. "We have a missing link."

"The police know?" he asked.

"Right now it's a Fire Marshall thing. The Fire Marshall is a friend of mine."

"Arson and bomb squads are your thing, aren't they?" Williams remarked. He knew about my earlier cases. "If you can keep our name out of it, I'd appreciate it. If you need help, give me a call. I have connections, if you get my drift. Mitch is going to be spending a few weeks here, getting to know the business. If you need something, just ask him."

As they left, the Captain and Gus drove up to us in a golf cart. "We've found the connection!" Gus exclaimed.

"Just before she died, Emily was excited that an old friend from Bryn Mawr was coming to visit her. She was planning big party," the Captain said. "Her friend, Eleanor, married an Englishman who hit the big time. He got knighted."

"We found the order for the engraved invitations," Gus said. "The nobleman was Sir Frederick Harter!"

"Well?" I asked. I had never heard of the man.

"England's foremost art historian," Gus went on. "He wrote *Art & Civilization*. It's the basic textbook for Introduction to Art History 101 across the nation. It's a good book, by the way, well written for the layman, but sophisticated."

"It was going to be a big party, almost everyone was going to be invited," the Captain explained.

"Someone would certainly say, "Oh sir Frederick, I have a Georges Seurat, or a Frederick Remington, or a Thomas Eakins hanging over my sofa, you must come to see it." Gus said.

"Is he was the guy who did the special, "Genius and Frauds" on PBS?" I asked. I remembered him now.

"That's the man," Gus said. "He made his reputation exposing some fake Vermeers. Sir Frederick must be well over 80 now. It would be a real coup to expose a fraud in his sunset years."

We now knew the motive for the murder and had suspects, but we hadn't closed the deal. I went to the employees' locker room. Larry had driven his own car so he could go out-of-town to a conference. I went by Glenn's office to see if he was ready. Joe Williams was with him.

"Sorry, I didn't know you were busy." I said.

"We're not busy at all, come on in," Glenn said, "I was just helping Joe with a bout of indigestion."

I entered the room. I had the feeling I had interrupted something. "Glenn's friend of mine," Joe said. "He said you were his friend too."

"I told Joe you are a popular guy," Glenn said. "Joe's really tense. He needs to relax more."

"Don't we all," I said. I glanced at the door to the back room. Glenn smiled and the three of us went to the former woman's locker. Glenn began to take of his clothes immediately. In his suit, Joe was commanding, naked he was uncomfortable. He was hairy, but not as hairy as Mitch. He had a linebackers build, but had gained weight.

When I looked him in the eye, he was looking down, directly at my cock. He quickly averted his eyes. I realized he was shy. I went over to him and put my arm around his shoulders. "Guys look all the time. I don't mind," I said. "We've all got the same basic equipment."

"It looks to me that you got the king sized version," he said.

"Don't worry," I said. "I share my toys and play well with others." We went to the cot on the side of the room. Joe got on it and I fed him my cock while Glenn sucked him. I somehow thought Joe was new to the scene, but he didn't suck that way. He was enthusiastic and skilled. Glenn began to rim Joe's ass so I leaned over and we sixty-nined.

It was no surprise when Glenn coated his cock in lubricant and began poking at Joe's rear entry. Glenn wasn't huge, but he had a nice piece of meat. Glenn was a playful fucker. He probed, pulsed, and pushed. He took his time and had fun on the way, but after five or six minutes his cock had vanished into Joe's rectum.

A cock is a lust thermometer. You can't fake an erection, precum, or an orgasm when a guy's sucking your cock. Joe was a shy, but very sensual man. His cock wasn't at all reserved. It liked everything Glenn and I did.

Glenn pulled out to catch his breath. I switched positions on the cot. I wasn't sure he could take mine, but I figured I give him the option. Joe had other ideas. He got Glenn on his hands and knees and then rear-ended him. Joe's cock was long and thin. Glen had no problem at all. I was pretty sure this wasn't the first time Joe had fucked Glenn. I would have been left out of this little scene, if Joe hadn't spread his legs and ass wide.

Joe had a bubble butt ass. Hair swirled around his ass cheeks, and his puffy hole was pink and pretty. Glenn's fucking left it juicy, and his stance meant there was no way to defend it. I heavily coated my cock with lubricant. I nosed my knob into his hole, grabbed him by the shoulders and pushed it in. He tried to resist for a split second, then he surrendered. It was a total, unconditional surrender. My entire cock slid into his ass.

As soon as my curly pubic hairs touched his ass, Joe tightened his buns and grasped my cock. I have some extra foreskin, so his sphincter held my skin, but my shaft and head were free to probe deeper. I held his shoulders tightly and pulled him back on to my cock. Joe shivered and moaned. I slipped still deeper in his love tunnel.

Somehow, I knew my knob was in unexplored virgin territory. I slowly pumped. Joe was purring like a satisfied cat. Life was good. It may sound odd, but sometimes I'm a regular Mother Theresa when it comes to fucking. My motives aren't as virtuous as hers were, but I like to do good deeds. I did a good deed for Joe. He went somewhere special. I don't know if it was nirvana, or heaven, but it was good. The bible doesn't say anything about getting the heaven by being fucked by a horse-hung, hairball, but that's what happened.

I felt the glow, so did Glen. We three were cock linked into a single fucking organism. I don't know how long we stayed that way, but I began to shoot. My first ejaculation was matched by Joe's a second later. Glen cried that he was shooting. It went on forever, or at least it seemed that way.

Part 8

"Is this a private party?" a deep voice asked. It was Mitch. I think Joe would have been shocked, if he had been capable of being shocked. Right now, he was still ejaculating. We were caught red handed, naked and dripping cum. By the time Joe was finished shooting, Mitch was naked. When I pulled out of Joe's ass, Mitch went in. Mitch's butt-plug style cock hit the spot.

"I didn't know you swung this way, Uncle Joe," Mitch said as he slowly pumped.

"I had no idea about you either," Joe said. "It feels really good." After the orgasm, Glenn and I were mellow and I didn't think there was much chance we would shoot again. Mitch was revved up. It was fun to watch him get it on with his uncle. They talked and discovered that what Mitch had interpreted as being disliked by his Uncle was Joe's worry about being found out.

Joe soon got hard again and he switched places with Mitch. Joe's cock was on the upper side of average in length and width. It was a perfect fit for Mitch's ass. I glanced at Glenn as they fucked. He was turned on big time. Working up to a second orgasm is time consuming, so Glenn tapped Joe on the shoulder and asked if he could cut in. Joe looked at Mitch. Mitch nodded and in a second, Glenn was making a call on Mitch's prostate.

It was a long session. Later I got on the bed and cradled Mitch in my arms as Glenn and Joe tag teamed him. Glenn and Joe traded places several times. With each penetration, the entrance was easier. The fuckers got harder and Mitch got more responsive. Glenn shot off first and Joe used his cum to lubricate his final thrusts. The second Joe's cock began to give his nephew's prostate a cum bath, Mitch popped. Joe shot most of his load on the dark side of Mitch's ass, but pulled out and squirted a few volleys on the quivering hole. Glenn was there to lick up Mitch's cock caviar as well as the remains of Joe's orgasm. He then moved to Mitch's ass and tongued it.

They broke apart.

The next day was quiet. Joe Williams had gone home leaving Mitch guarding the fort. Mitch seemed like a clunky a kid, but I saw him talking to Henry. I didn't think Henry was his type, so I assumed he was doing what his Uncle had told him. I also didn't think Mitch was Henry's cup of tea, but being the nephew of the boss would be enough for Henry. By lunchtime, they were pals. I saw Tiffany looking at them with disapproval.

Gus and the Captain were still visiting residents and I could tell they had really hit it off. I was wondering if the Captain was looking for a permanent nephew. Back in Richmond, Jonathan had caught R. Winston's fancy and was working part-time at the gallery. He told me he was going to a weekend party at R. Winston's river house and he thought it was going to be good.

I was going to see my art historian friends on Saturday. Gus had taken pictures of the suspect paintings and would have them ready for me to show the professionals. Elliot was out-of-town, but Sedgwick was available. Gus and the Captain drove into town and we went to Sedgwick's apartment. Sedgwick knew of Gus as a sculptor, but hadn't met him. Gus and the Captain had done their homework on the paintings. The Captain had a good memory and had written down the stories used to hook the Essex Park residents. When you saw it in black and white, the scheme was well thought out. Most of the stories were based on newspaper or magazine articles of the last few years.

They were the sort of stories a person casually interested in art might have seen. All dealt with recently discovered works that had been lost, or forgotten. They were purchased by unsuspecting persons, who discovered the true significance of the painting and all made a mint. One of the paintings had been brought over by a G.I. who picked it up on a World War II battlefield. Another had been given to a cook from the Adirondacks who had worked for Remington.

The stories were credible to the casual observer. The most expensive of the paintings was $75,000.00, the most economical was $15,000.00. In each case, there was a reason why the painting was going for such a bargain. In one case, a widow needed cash for an operation. R. Winston inferred the provenance of one or two of the paintings were slightly off.

Sedgwick had been doing his own investigations. R. Winston Jones had been Randall W. Jones when he ran a gallery in Miami. There he had gone after millionaires for big bucks and had come perilously close to serving time in the big house.

"How did he get away with it?" I asked.

"There was a sexual component," Sedgwick explained. "His customers were happily married closet cases who liked a little fun on the side. Randall was younger and thinner then and had no problem taking a trip on the wild side. He likes it kinky. It was easier for everyone if no one pressed charges."

I went to the phone and called Jonathan. I thought he might like to know something about R. Winston's sexual tastes. Jonathan wasn't worried. "I can go with the flow," he told me.

Sedgwick, Gus and Captain hit it off well. The art historical talk was a bit beyond my conversational level, but when the discussion turned to fraud, I was a happy camper. We had figured out the outline of the scam. The murder still remained a puzzle. It seemed to me it was easier for R. Winston to leave town than to kill an elderly lady. Forgery and fraud are bad, but not bad enough to justify murder. I had a feeling we were missing something.

I got a call on my cell phone and went to another room to take it. It was about another case and I make a point not to talk in public, even among friends. When I returned the room was empty. I could sniff the smell of sexual excitement. I went looking for the men. They were in the kitchen in a group grope. Everyone must have realized we were all like spirits and the night was young.

"This may sound tacky, but if we're going to grope each other let's get naked and do it right," I said. We went to Sedgwick's bedroom and got naked. After a little confusion, I ended up with Gus' cock in my mouth. He was uncut and meaty. The Captain and Sedgwick were in the 69 position on the bed.

My knees hurt, so I got up and Gus went down on my cock. "Damn, it is big," Gus said. "I've never been this close." At first, he didn't seem to know what to do with it, but he figured it out. A little later Sedgwick came over to me when the Captain played with Gus.

I suspected Sedgwick wanted to be fucked and I was in the mood too. I didn't know if Gus and the Captain would mind, but they were big boys. They could deal with it.

I sucked Sedgwick and worked a finger into his ass. Sedgwick relaxed as soon as my finger touched his hole. He wanted it. I'm not into pent up sexual needs much. Some guys tell me they've been without sex for months and were looking for just the right guy. For me the right guy has a cock, an asshole and good attitude. I do admit, as I get older the right attitude gets more important. I've had some good times with guys who didn't turn me on. It's been good as long as they're into it.

The first time I had screwed Sedgwick it had been a lot of work. It was easier this time. Sedgwick's bedroom was small, so there was no way for Gus and the Captain not to watch. They were both enthusiastic and helpful. They gave Sedgwick support and added lube when it was needed. Gus fed Sedgwick his cock when he needed some inspiration. The Captain licked up Sedgwick's cock drool.

I'm not much of an asshole man. Cocks excite me. Assholes are necessary if you're going to fuck a guy, but not pretty. Gus liked assholes. He really got off on watching my cock stretch Sedgwick open and then push deep. He later told me he had never watched a guy get fucked up close and personal.

I take my time. I took a while to pop the sphincter with my knob. I like to tenderize it. Sedgwick was a passionate and demonstrative man. Gus watched me and saw what each movement did to Sedgwick. Gay porn usually gives a sanitary and prissy view of fucking. Sedgwick had a hairy ass, and a hole that opened more and more as he got more excited. His ass hairs stuck to my cock when I pulled out, and when I pushed in the hair went in too. His rosebud and ass linings were all visible and a few times the hole didn't have time to close up before I went in again. Gus liked that a lot and was turned on.

I don't think the Captain had Gus's interest in assholes, but he did get excited when Gus was excited. I knew they were attracted to each other and I had a feeling sex between them was good, but careful. You can be timid when you are hoping for a relationship. The Captain now realized their relationship could be both tender and much more sexual.

The night was a success for all of us. I got home late and actually slept later. When I woke up, I had a nice lazy day doing nothing. At five, Jonathan came back from his party at R. Winston's river house.

Jonathan had an adventure with R. Winston. The weekend party was a combination of young oriental and Latino boys, and older men who wanted them. Jonathan spoke Spanish, so he knew what some the boys were up too. "As far as I can tell, the boys were available for rent or sale. Some of the older men were sugar daddies, but there were several pure unadulterated sickos," Jonathan explained. "I did meet one nice guy there. Rich was R. Winston's next-door neighbor. He seemed normal."

"Did you have a problem ?" I asked, " I hadn't planned for you to get in that far."

"I can take care of myself. To tell you the truth I had some fun on the side." Jonathan said. "There was a double scam going on. R. Winston was selling Oriental and Mexican virgin boys. The boys were older than they looked and had a hard life. They wanted to get to the U.S.A. and getting fucked by few old geezers was a small price to pay."

"R. Winston is a real humanitarian," I said.

"He's into water sports and bondage," Jonathan continued. "He likes sadism, but I think it's mostly of the theatrical sort. It's 90% play acting."

"And the 10%?" I asked.

"Nothing that leaves a mark on the body," Jonathan. "He's hung and doesn't mind forcing it in. If the hole's not big enough he can make it wider. He's not the gentle type. I'd classify it as a rape, but the boys see it as an initiation. They're all illegal, so he has them by the short hairs."

"Did he try to rape you?"

"Not until later. I'm way too old for him," Jonathan said. "I'm also English speaking, and an adult. R. Winston is cagey. By the way, there's a camera in one of the bedrooms."

"Let me guess. It's the room where the older men go to play?"

"Bingo!"

"I found the camera by accident. I guess it's either an insurance policy, or it may be his retirement plan," Jonathan observed. "It was well hidden. It's run from R. Winston's bedroom."

"You did get around," I said.

"R. Winston fell asleep," Jonathan said. "I kind of stretched his ass a little wider."

"Did he complain?"

"At first, but he came around," Jonathan said. "Usually I'm not much of a top, but I hit the bull's eye and our friend couldn't breathe let alone think."

"I thought he wasn't into older men?"

Jonathan laughed. "He's into sales. He had the boys with customers so only Rich and I were available. Rich found an older playmate, so R. Winston was stuck with me. He tried to jump me. I did the quick switcher-roo on him. He's a big guy and didn't realize I'm stronger than I look. He didn't know what hit him. Actually, he didn't realize what grabbed him. He's has big balls. They are low hangers too, easy to grab, twist and crush if necessary."

"It wasn't necessary?"

"He came around pretty quickly," Jonathan said. "Once my cock was in his ass he was a whimpering mass of begging crap. He's a big man, but his ass is tight. I forced it in. Unfortunately, the harder I pushed, the harder he got. That wasn't what I was after, but that's life. When he shot off, he fell asleep. I had a chance to look around, then I got dressed and went home. Rich gave me a ride. We had some fun too. It was a good weekend, but I don't think I be interning there on Monday."

That night I Googled art fraud. I got way too many hits. I tried art fraud, China. That was more reasonable. I tried a few links, but they were all related to Chinese antiquities. I tried western painting, forgery and Chinese. I got a reasonable number of hits. I went through them in order, then went to the second page of hits. Midway down the list I found a reference to the *China Queen*. I remembered the *China Queen* was a container ship involved in a news story. When they opened one of the containers there were eighteen dead Chinese men. They had been abandoned and all died from the heat. It was a big scandal at the time.

No one was convicted of the crime since none of the owners could be traced. The ship itself had gone back to China by the time the bodies were discovered. When they found the ship, it had an all new crew and captain. The dead Chinese were all young men and boys desperate to get to America. The article mentioned the container also held boxes of reproduction paintings. This wasn't emphasized in the article. I called Vince DeSoto. He remembered the *China Queen* incident. It was treated as problem related to illegal immigration. He hadn't noticed the mention of the boxes of paintings.

"I bet everyone thought the paintings are incidental," Vince said. "You wouldn't connect an immigrant smuggling operation with a forged painting scam, would you?"

"Maybe it's a coincidence," I said, "but that's what we seem to have at Essex Park. Eighteen dead men would provide a good motive for murder."

"Maybe eighteen Chinese men and one elderly American woman died," Vince said. "I'll check up on this."

I called one of my Internet gurus, Walter, and asked him to do a complete search on the *China Queen* incident. Walter was a retired librarian who was obsessive, complete and fast. He called me at ten that night and gave me a preliminary report.

"Very unsavory," he said. "White washed by the press and by the complimentary concerns of the Chinese and American governments. It represented a gigantic lapse in port security. The *China Queen* docked in Baltimore in the middle of a security crackdown. This crackdown was listed by the President as evidence the port security operations were successful. Oddly no one mentioned when or where the ship docked."

"The eighteen men were all gay and many had arrests for prostitution," Walter continued. "China does not like to admit it has a gay community. You may recall this was at a time when one of those odd television evangelists was claiming the Mexicans were exporting their gay AIDS victims to the US to infect us. That man knew nothing about God, not to mention any passing acquaintance with human decency. Anyway, the Chinese government wanted nothing to do with the story."

"So no one looked?"

"No one official looked," Walter replied.

"Did you find out anything about the paintings?"

"The boxes were labeled as belonging to the Renaissance Art Company. They had a false address. The recipients address was torn off. One scrap remained with the initials R.W.J. Does that mean anything to you?"

"Yes it does," I said, "It could mean a lot."

Part 9

Things were moving along at a good pace. While I didn't have proof, I had found a motive good enough to murder an elderly woman. I had no idea how to smoke out the bad guys.

I gave this information to Mitch, Gus and the Captain over drinks. Mitch called his Uncle about my suspicions. Joe didn't like where this was going. It was a nightmare for him. He had spent much of his life cleaning up his family's association with the mob. This went up in smoke if this crime was associated with the deaths on the *China Queen*.

"I know how we can force the issue," the Captain said. "I can invite Sir Frederick and Eleanor Harter to Essex Park. We can say it's to pay respects or something like that. I could have Emily's cocktail party. That would get the ball rolling again and smoke them out."

"That would do the trick," Gus said. "It might be dangerous though."

"I can take care of myself," the Captain said.

"Would Sir Frederick do it?" I asked.

"He wouldn't need to do it. We just need to say we will have him here," Captain Green said. "I can contact him and see if he would allow us to say that."

The phone rang. The Captain answered it and we heard half the conversation. "Yes, Larry," he said.

"Oh my God. How is he?"

"Dead! You're kidding! What happened?" There was a long gap as Larry told the Captain what he knew.

"Yes, Mitch is here," he said as he handed the phone to Mitch. Larry repeated the same information to Mitch.

"Jon's dead. He skidded off the road. The car exploded when he hit a tree," the Captain said. "They say he died instantly. The explosion was just icing on the cake."

Someone knocked on the door. It was Glen with the same news.

"I don't like this at all," I said. "Sometimes an accident is just an accident, but this worries me."

"Jon drove the residents on trips. He was the most cautious man I know. Knew, I mean," Glenn said. "I can't see him skidding on a road. I can't see him going fast enough to skid."

Mitch hung up and was now calling his uncle on his cell phone. That conversation went on for a while. After he hung up he said, "I'm going to be in charge here. Uncle Joe is coming down the day after tomorrow. He can't get out of a meeting tomorrow." He paused. "Who can I trust to help me? Henry and Tiffany aren't on my kissy-kissy list."

"Larry," Glenn, the Captain and I said almost simultaneously.

As if on cue, Larry appeared at the door. Mitch told him of Joe's plan and asked if Larry could help.

"Sure, I'd be glad to do what I can. We have to tell the residents. I think we're a little young to be reassuring. I was wondering if Captain Green could help. I was thinking about an e mail, or a message on our closed circuit television system, but that doesn't seem right."

"It's six now, why don't we send out a message on the TV, then have a meeting at 8:00," Captain Green suggested. "We can call it a memorial event, so we don't need to explain too much."

"I can get that done. I arranged for Mrs. Carlisle's memorial," Larry said. Mitch, Larry and the Captain went off to arrange things. I went with Glenn to his office. Glenn agreed with me it was more than a coincidence. I called Vince and told him about Jon and the accident. He said he'd check into it.

Vince had been around for years and was intelligent, thorough and helpful. When a trooper needed some information quickly, Vince obliged. He could find out what the cops really thought had happened to Jon.

He called me back an hour later. "The word is the accident was a sloppy effort to hide a murder. I told them to check for sleeping pills. They liked that idea a lot," he said. "I also asked them to keep it an accident as long as possible. Tommy Wilson was in charge. Do you know him?"

I said no. He continued, "Tommy's a good, hardworking and sensible man. He not the brightest man in the world, but he's no fool. He wanted to know if this was a big deal. I told him I thought it might be, but he would get credit for it if credit were due. He understood. By the way, this is strictly amateur night, no professional hit man here."

"Maybe it's a spur of the minute event?"

"That could be," Vince remarked as he hung up.

Mrs. Julia Denton, Jon's secretary, came in the office, obviously distraught. She was having palpitations and was almost in shock. She was a middle-aged lady who was my image of the perfect secretary. Glenn gave her a pill and had her sit down. The phone began ringing off the hook. Glenn asked me to sit with her until the drug took effect.

She was a little afraid of me, but Glenn told her I was better than I looked. We sat on a bench outside. The fresh air made me feel better. "How long had you been with Mr. Dustin?" I asked. I hoped talking about him would help her.

"Seven years, he was a perfect gentleman and so kind," she sobbed. "When my husband died he couldn't have been more kind and helpful. He helped everyone who needed it. You wouldn't believe how patient he was. So many of the residents can be a trial, but he never got mad or aggravated." Once she started reciting his list of virtues, she calmed down. I asked if I could take her pulse. She said yes, and then resumed her tribute to Jon Dustin.

"He had been so worried after Mrs. Carlisle's death," she said. "I told him there was no way to protect the residents from their own short comings." She looked at me. "You know many of them aren't as sharp as they use to be." I nodded. "He got very worried after I gave him the program."

"What program was that?" I asked.

"My son, Spencer, is a software programmer. He developed a program called Administrator Cop. It's for network administrators to check for private use of the company network," she explained. "It's not quite ready for beta testing, but it's close."

"What does it do?"

"Well, if you're the network administrator, it will search out password protected users and break the password," she said. "Spencer is so bright. I got a copy for Jon, I mean Mr. Dustin, to try out. Mr. Dustin was good with computers. Well, he took it into his office and when he came out an hour later, he was white as a sheet. I thought the program had crashed the network or something like that. I said, "Oh no, the program didn't work?"

"He said, "No, the program works too well." I was relieved."

"That must have been a relief to you," I said, "Your son wouldn't have given you a program with a bug in it, would he?"

"You are right about that, but you always worry, don't you?"

I agreed with her and then asked, "What did Mr. Dustin do next?"

"He went down the hall to Henry's office," she said. "I had to go home early. The ladies of the church were serving trays for the church night dinner, so I don't know when he got out of his meeting with Henry."

"When did you give him the program?" I asked.

"About a week ago," Mrs. Danton said. I took her pulse again and it was almost normal. By now, residents were heading toward the dining room and an elderly couple came over to us and took her to the service.

The meeting was subdued; the residents were shocked. Jon had been good to them and they appreciated all that he did. It was over by nine. Tiffany and Henry were out-of-town at a convention. Mitch wanted Larry and Glenn to stay there for the night. Some of the residents were excited and scared. Glenn had driven that day, so I was stuck there too. Mitch was staying at one of those suite-type hotels a half mile away, so he offered to put us up for the night. Mitch wanted things to look normal, but he wanted to be nearby in case something happened. Billy

Fillmore had his regular security people on duty, and they would call us. Fillmore also brought in some additional people to give some extra protection. I asked him to make sure no one was doing anything in the office area.

Glenn, Larry and I went off to Mitch's suite. He had a modest bedroom and sitting room, but the suite had a spectacular bath. It had a Jacuzzi and a walk-in shower. Mitch, Glen, Larry and I may have beaten the world record for getting naked and in to the shower. Larry may not have known Mitch's sexual preferences, but Larry had no problem being naked in front of other men. I filled the Jacuzzi and we all got in after it had filled. By then Larry and Mitch were erect and knew the lay of the land. Glenn and I played the elder statesmen for the younger men. The bubbling water hid groping hands.

We were all tired and stressed and this proved to be a recipe for fun. Everyone wanted to get some sleep after some hot, ball draining sex. Usually four men turn into two couples, but not this night. I didn't want to limit myself to one man or one cock. I wanted them all and I think they felt the same way. Larry sat on the edge of the tub. Glenn and Mitch shared the young man's cock. I was on the other side so I got in the water and fingered Glenn and Mitch's holes. Mitch moaned when my finger reached his prostate.

I took my finger out and inserted my thumb. This let me grasp their asses and both apply pressure on their prostate and lift them slightly from the water. I thought this might distract them from Larry's cock, but they kept their eyes on the prize. Larry looked at me and smiled. He may not have known Mitch yet, but now he knew we were all like spirits.

We got out of the whirlpool and got on the bed. Mitch's room was fully equipped for a fun night. He pulled out an overnight case with lubricant and poppers. He and Larry got on the bed in the 69 position and went at it hot and heavy. I handed Glenn and tube of lube and took a tube for myself. Touched Larry's ass and he opened up. Glenn did the same with Mitch. They both knew they were going to be fucked and were willing.

As we lubricated opened our respective bottom's asses, they got more excited. When you're sucking the cock of a guy who's being fucked, you have a front row and center seat. My horse cock popped through Larry's ass as the beefy nurse poked into Mitch's behind. We were four happy men.

The four of us formed a sex machine. My cock was like a piston ramming deep into Larry's ass. Mitch was deep throating Larry's cock. When he engulfed the entire cock, he was an inch from the asshole and my cock. He watched me fuck and tasted Larry react. Glancing at Glen I saw he was thrusting in when I was pulling out.

"Let's make this last," I said. We broke apart and got back into the tub. When we got out the next time, Glenn and Mitch sixty-nined. Larry took care of Mitch and I popped Glenn. I knew Glenn wanted to be fucked, but wasn't sure about my cock. He didn't need to worry. A lot of lubricant and a few snorts of poppers did the trick. Once I was in, he relaxed, Glenn was a perfect bottom pig. We were friends, but his ass was in love with my cock.

Larry was a size or two bigger than Glenn was and it took some time to skewer Mitch on his meat. Once it was in, I saw some signs of true love. Larry seemed to like to pop his head through the sphincter, using it to massage his head. When he pushed deep however, Mitch shivered. Larry would pop his head in and out of the hole several times and then ram hard. Both men got what they wanted. They were well matched.

We broke apart and returned to the tub. For the third go around, Glenn and I sucked each other while Mitch and Larry fucked us. That was good too. Larry began by screwing me, and then he switched to take Glenn.

Mitch's butt plug shaped cock was both effective and fun to watch. It was hard to believe Glenn's ass could open wide enough to take it, but it did. When it was my turn it barely fit, but was worth the effort. Mitch began the grand finale when he shot his load in my ass. His moans induced Larry to climax and he rear loaded Glenn. When Larry pulled out, he was still hard. He mounted me doggy style and we had an intense but short pile driver in heat episode. I couldn't tell if he had a second orgasm, or just finished the one he started in Glenn's ass. We all fell asleep on the king sized bed.

We got a call at 5:30 that they needed Glenn. The three of us dozed off again. When I finally woke up, Larry and Mitch were making out again. I went to the bath and showered. When I returned Mitch was slow fucking Larry. Mitch's butt- plug style cock worked its magic on Larry's prostate.

Mitch got a call from Essex Park and we went back to the development. I had a chance to call into the office. I asked them to keep a close eye on R. Winston and the gallery and asked if they had any information on Tiffany. The dispatcher told me to call back at noon.

I walked from the locker room to the main office and ran into Mrs. Danton. She was with a younger man. She greeted me as an old friend and introduced me to her son Spencer. Spencer was disheveled, bearded and somehow I knew he was a Star Trek fan. He was that type.

"I told Mom she should take the day off, but she insisted on going to work," he said.

"There are arrangements to be made," she said. "I know what he would like." Captain Green saw us and came over. He told her he was working on the memorial service and needed her help if she could manage. Mrs. Danton was a happy to be needed as they went to the office.

"Spencer, your mother told me about a program you are developing," I said. "Apparently Jon used it and found something disturbing. Could you look in the network here and see what you can find?"

"Sure. Why are you interested?" he asked.

"I mentioned it to one of the management guys and he wanted to know more," I replied.

"Mr. Dustin's death was really unexpected. Wasn't it?" he asked suspiciously. I didn't say anything. "He was a timid driver, as I recall." Spencer knew something was a foot. We went in the office. I introduced him to Mitch and Larry. Mitch was into computers and they went off to tryout the new program.

The phone was ringing off the hook, but Mrs. Danton was efficient and fast. She had another secretary, Alice, answering the phone. She would send an instant message to Mrs. Danton who would take the call if it were important; Alice handled all the normal calls. Both women wore headsets so they could type and send emails. Mrs. Danton worked out the funeral and memorial details with the Captain and Larry. Now that she had something to do, she was over the shock of the death. She and the Captain became Julia and Will. They had bonded.

They were off getting some sandwiches for lunch and I was manning the phone when I got a call from Sir Frederick Harter for the Captain. I explained he was away at lunch. He said he was on his way to a lecture and wouldn't be back for several hours. "I tried to call our friend Emily Carlisle, but the phone was disconnected.

I gave him the bad news. He was shocked. He was still planning to visit Essex Park in a week. I told him of the circumstances surrounding Emily's murder. Sir Frederick may have been a distinguished art historian, but in an earlier life he must have been an avenging angel. His wife wasn't with him because of dementia. He hated art forgers and despised those who took advantage of the elderly. I told him of the Captain's plan for a party. "Well, if this scum is worried about being discovered, I'm the man to give them real heartburn," he said.

"We may have a second murder," I said. "We think the director of the place may have discovered something. He had an accident."

"I'm 82 years old," he said. "I'm not going to die young." I got his phone number and said the Captain would call him that evening.

Will and Julia returned with sandwiches for me and for Mitch and Spencer. Spencer had cracked the passwords, but both Henry and Tiffany had erased their files. This had annoyed Spencer. He wasn't annoyed they had erased the files; he was annoyed their efforts were so pathetic. Several had actually been erased, but the e-mail program maintained an address book, and all the senders names were on the list. I asked him to send the names to Vince so he could check them on the police computers.

Spencer wanted to hack into the police computers himself, but I talked him out of that. He sent the info to Vince. Mitch came in and told me his Uncle was on his way. He asked if I could meet him at the airport at 7:00. Jon's children were going to be arriving at Essex Park and he thought he should meet them. I got a change of clothes in the locker room and took an Essex Park car to the airport. Joe got in a half hour late. He had his accountant with him, Roy. Roy may have been an accountant, but he could have passed for a bouncer for a down and dirty Country & Western bar. He was a bruiser.

I gave them the low down and told them about Spencer's discoveries. Roy wasn't a friendly guy, but he warmed up as I went over the situation. Audits were normal when there was an event of this sort. I said I doubted there was a problem with Jon's bookkeeping.

"I'll check anyway," Roy said, "I can find other ways to occupy my time if I need to." I took them to the office. Joe went off to meet Jon's family. I took Roy to Mrs. Danton's office and stayed with him. It turned out Roy had electronic copies of all the records back at the main office. He was looking for other documents. As I expected, Jon's had correctly filed all his records. We moved on to Henry's office. Roy put on gloves and did an orderly and complete police-type search of the office. He looked in every nook and cranny of the office, including the undersides of drawers, lamps and the rear of pictures. Unlike the police, he put everything back in place afterward. I stood shotgun at the door.

I got the printout of Henry and Tiffany's e-mail addresses. Roy looked as if Christmas had come early. I scanned it and sent it to his office. It was 10:00 before he was finished.

"Can you take me to the hotel?" he asked. We went to the hotel where Mitch had been staying. "Do you mind waiting for Joe to come back?" he asked, "He wants to talk." I agreed. We went to his room and he ordered room service dinners for me, Joe and Mitch. The dinners arrived a half-hour later with Mitch and Joe. We ate and Mitch went off to his room. He was to meet with the family early the next morning to work on funeral arrangements.

I called Vince. He said they found sedatives in Jon's body. The dosage was such that he could not possibly have been driving. They were working their way through the e-mail addresses. When I went back to the room, Joe and Roy were gone. The communicating door to the next room was open. I looked into the next room and saw Joe with a highball lying on the bed in his boxers, and Roy was making another drink wearing his birthday suit.

"Is this a private party?" I asked.

"It is, but you're the guest of honor," Joe replied. Just once in my life I would like to be given a choice between sex and getting some much needed sleep and pick the rest. As usual, my cock made the choice for me.

Part 10

Joe, Roy and I made an odd trio. I was half Joe's size and a third of Roy's. Roy was huge, not just tall, but massive.

"If one of you guys rolls over, I'm a dead man," I said.

"I've never killed anyone by accident yet," Roy said. He had a shaved head and body. His cock looked average, but that may have been in comparison to his massive bulk. His balls were huge.

I cupped them in my hand. "Are the full?" I asked.

"Shit yes," he replied. "Are you into cream?"

"I've got no problem with home brewed man cream, as long as it's fresh from the balls," I answered. That was what he wanted to hear.

"Are you a top?" he asked.

"Most of the time," I said.

"So am I," Roy replied. "Is that a problem for you?"

"I kind of doubt it," I said. "I'm a pretty open minded man."

"Is your ass open too?"

"For you it would be," I said. "What about your ass?"

"Not usually, but I can be inspired," Roy said. "Joe and I don't get out much were we can let out hair down, so to speak." I was tired, but I revived as the sexual tension intensified. Roy wasn't what you would call the sensitive lover type. He knew what he wanted and intended to get it. "Why don't you get naked and we can have some fun?" That was fine for me.

While Roy wasn't the sensitive type he did share some basic curiosity. When he saw my cock, he was interested. "Joe, you told me you took this fucker?" he asked.

"I sure did," Joe replied.

"I didn't know you were into that," Roy said. Roy dropped to the floor to get a better look at my organ. He took a few licks and decided he liked it. He also licked a finger and went for my ass. He had meaty long fingers and found my prostate in record time. When the first finger fit, he added a second.

"Don't hog him," Joe complained. "Bring him over so we can share." Roy picked me up and carried me to the bed. I am not picked up often, but this was the first time a guy was gripping me by my ass. He had a finger on each side of my prostate and it was a wild sensation. When he got me to the bed, he deposited me face down into Joe's crotch. I began to suck it when Roy lifted my ass and spread my ass so he could fuck me doggy style.

A second or two later his well-lubricated cock popped into my ass. After his fingers, his blunt knob felt good. The head was a big mushroom, but the shaft was thin. I liked being cock head fucked so it was good for me. Roy briefly pumped me like a wild man, but soon slowed his pace. I knew he had gotten a lot closer to popping than he wanted at this early point. It was nice to know he could control himself.

Joe was leaking faster than a 30-year-old faucet. I don't mind being fucked from each end and all three of us were enjoying it. Roy pulled out, straddled Joe's face and fed him his balls. He also grabbed Joe's legs and spread them. He wanted me to fuck his boss. There was a tube of lubricant on the bed, so I took care of Joe's ass and them my cock.

"Let me see him take it!" Roy demanded. Joe's hole was quivering. I tested the hole with a few thrusts then went deep. There was damn little resistance. Joe's cock spurted a glob of cock juice. It wasn't pre cum, but the milky stuff. Joe had good self-control too.

Roy's cock was looking fully inflated. "You amaze me Joe," Roy whispered. "This is fucking beautiful! How can you take that mother fucker?" Roy moved so he could get a better look. He told me to pull out and then to fuck Joe deep. I did, and he loved it. "Look at those ass lips opening up? It's like a snake swallowing something twice its size."

Roy wasn't just a passive observer. He licked the cock drool from Joe's cock and then asked me to fuck Joe again. At first, I thought Roy was into humiliation, but that wasn't it. It was as if he was watching a great athlete testing his limits.

I pulled out to give Joe a rest. Roy took my place in the quivering asshole. "You are beautiful baby," he said. "I could never do that. You took it like a champ. It was beautiful." He paused. "Shit, I'm shooting." Roy twitched fifteen or twenty times as he rear loaded Joe. The warm cream flooding his ass must have been too much Joe. His cock went off like a Roman candle. Both men collapsed on the bed and were asleep in seconds. I went to sleep myself.

The next day I had a run in with Tiffany for the first time. She saw me cleaning up the beds near the dining room. "For a new man, a lot of people seem to know you," she said.

"You know ma'am, I'm short and I'm ugly. People seem to remember me," I said. "Logically speaking, I'm the kind of guy you'd want to forget. It's a puzzlement." I think she would have smiled at that, but she was afraid her face would crack.

"I heard you were hanging out with Mr. Williams," she said.

"Hanging out is a nice way to put it," I said. "Running errands and doing chores is more correct. I speak English too. He doesn't like using the high priced staff to do shit work. Most of the economy priced staff is Mexican."

"I don't know why he's hanging around here," she observed as she walked away.

The memorial service for Jon was good. His children and parents were there. Jon's kids were 12, 14 and 19 and the residents were more than kind and sympathetic to them. His parents seemed dazed. Glenn told me the ex-wife had outed Jon to them. They were born-agains and took it badly. Now it was too late. Julia helped them. I recognized several men as detectives in plain clothes. Several others I suspected were Feds of some sort. The minister who had done Mrs. Carlisle's funeral was back and was good.

He did a sermon on sudden death and the natural regret that you never had a chance to say good-bye. "There is no chance to say you're sorry. No way to ask for forgiveness for those things that seem so petty now that Jon is dead," he said. " God knows all and makes all things known. Words are unnecessary. God will make all things good and whole." I had no desire to let the parents off that lightly. My mom, however, would have told me not to be an asshole, although that wasn't the word she would have used. She wasn't much into revenge. The Captain gave a nice remembrance of Jon. He pulled together all of the kindnesses he had done for the residents and all the comical interludes. This lightened the mood.

There was a buffet lunch after the service. I watched Henry and Tiffany make kissy-face with several of the residents. I detected a trace of unease in them. I also noticed one or two of the men I thought were Feds were watching them too.

After lunch, the Grand Parents took the younger kids home with them, but the 19-year-old boy was heading back to college in Philadelphia. The Grandparents were going west to West Virginia. They didn't like to drive in the dark and were scared of city driving. The boy, Jon Jr., had been talking with Glenn. Glen offered to drop him off at the Richmond train station.

Jon Jr. was a slimmer, younger version of his father. He was attentive and almost fatherly to his two younger sisters. He was the man of the family now. It was apparent there had been bad blood between the grandparents and the kids, but the grandparents were desperately trying to make amends.

Glenn, Jon and I went to Richmond. We were almost in Richmond when the radio reported there was a major train wreck near Baltimore. Train service was halted until the next morning. We went to my apartment to regroup.

In the car, I noticed Glenn and Jon had really hit it off. I had a suspicion Jon shared his father's sexual tastes. Jon seemed to have good gaydar for a kid his age. He had figured out the lay of the land. I made some calls to see what the situation heading north. It was bad everywhere. There were thunderstorms screwing up the airlines and a tractor-trailer accident on I-95. Waiting for the next day was the logical course of action.

Jon and Glenn had disappeared when I got back to the living area. I heard the shower going. I went to my bedroom and found them undressing. "Jon just saw your shower and we're going to give it a spin." Glenn said.

"It looks like something out of some Caribbean resort," Jon said. By then Glenn had dropped his jockeys. He was half-erect. Jon saw that and did a double take. He looked at me. I was smiling, then he dropped his boxers. Jon was well beyond half-hard. They went into the shower. For a little while, I thought I'd leave them to their own devices, but then I figured what the hell. I stripped naked and joined them.

The party was already under way in the shower. Jon's mouth was firmly attached to Glenn's cock. His eyes and my eyes met. He had found the Holy Grail and was drinking from it. Unless my eyes deceived me, he also had a finger exploring Glenn's ass. Maybe Jon wasn't a complete virgin after all. I later found out that while Jon wasn't a virgin, he wasn't experienced either. His knowledge of gay sex was limited to restroom and shower room encounters. He also had one or two visits to adult bookstores.

His adventure in the shower of my apartment was the first time he had ever had sex without being afraid someone would catch him. I'm not much into young guys. I don't like breaking a guy in. Given that Jon must have come from the most conventional family background ever I thought it might be a shock for him to encounter two older gay men with enough sexual experience for ten or twenty men.

I was wrong about Jon. He was ripe, indeed over ripe. The only problem was that Jon seemed to shoot off at the drop of a hat. That was the bad news. The good news was that never got less than half-hard and his recharge time was ten to twelve minutes. Over the next twelve hours, he must have shot off maybe twenty times. He had a cock in his mouth, or up his ass most of the time. His cock tickled my tonsils a few times, but mostly it took up residence in Glenn's mouth or ass.

Jon was a sexual sponge, soaking up experience. There was nothing he wasn't interested in, or wasn't willing to try. Jon's body was pink and pale. With blond hair, not even his bush showed up. His tits were only a slightly more intense shade pink. He was toned. I guessed he was a runner, but he still looked young.

Jon loved Glenn's cock, but sucked on me too. Glenn has a pretty cock and balls. His shaft is smooth and his head a nice shiny pink. His slit is small and once and a while a little bead of precum appears. Glenn's bush is trimmed and neat. My cock is veiny with some extra foreskin. My wide slit is usually drooling. Usually there's a day's worth of man ooze stored in the skin. For the novice it can seem a bit gamy.

Jon got into it quickly. I later found out he had never sucked an uncut man before. After a while, we got out of the shower and went to my bed. We made a small daisy chain and when it was his time to suck me, he had no problem at all. When fully erect his cock was bigger than I had guessed. Glenn hadn't been able to deep throat him. I had no problem at all. Jon loved that. Glenn likes to rim, so as I swallowed Jon's cock, Glenn tongue fucked him. That little experiment resulted in a mouth full of cum for me.

Jon had a classic smooth baby's butt with a pretty little pink rosebud in the middle. It seemed to me it was too pretty to fuck. Glenn, however, was in a fucking mood. He gave Jon a little demonstration by fucking me. I enjoyed it. Then he gave Jon a chance to try me out. Jon was too ready for my ass. He shot off a few seconds after he pushed through my sphincter. We waited ten minutes and tried it a second time. This time, it was an unmitigated success for him and for me.

Jon and Glenn took turns screwing me. That was better than I expected. My ass was juicy after all the lube and cum. apparently I was a good advertisement to the joys of anal sex. Glenn talked Jon into trying the bottom. I lubricated Jon's hole. He jumped as I touched his ass. He was tight too, but after a little work I got two fingers in and eventually a third. Glenn was big and I wanted Jon to be ready.

"Are you going to get it all in?" Jon asked Glenn.

"There's no such thing as a semi virgin," Glenn said. "In a minute or two, your ass is either going to be 100% virgin, or 100% fucked." Jon smiled; he understood the rules.

I held Jon's legs open and Glenn stepped up to the plate. I like a slow fuck for a maiden voyage. Glen was a throw them in the water and see if they swim kind of man. I had lubricated Jon well. In one thrust, Jon wasn't a virgin. The cock winded Jon, but soon he was taking it like a man. When Glenn's probe made a bull's eye hit on Jon's prostate, he is eyes crossed. From his reactions I'm sure he didn't know he had a sex organ there.

Glenn pulled out to give Jon a breather. Jon was in my ass a few seconds later. He seemed more enthusiastic now that he had some idea what I was feeling. I was on the bed with my legs on Jon's shoulders when Glenn made an attack from the rear. The second penetration was totally unexpected so Jon was relaxed. By the time Jon knew Glenn was behind him, he was fucked. When Glenn said you have to be virgin or 100% fucked, I don't think Jon realized the full ramifications. He did now.

Jon loved it, all of it. The three of us were linked, cock to ass, and it was good for all of us. Somehow, we fit anatomically and the double fuck worked. It was five minutes before Glen shot his load into Jon and Jon sent another load into my hole. We pulled apart and caught our breath.

Jon talked about his father. They had a good relationship and the divorce had been hard on them. While Jon Jr. knew his father's sexual preference was the official reason for the breakup, his mother had another man waiting in the wings, so he wasn't sure. His mother was a difficult woman.

"Did Dad know you guys?" Jon asked.

"Don't ask the question if you don't want to know the answer," Glen said.

"I would like to know," Jon said. "I was hoping he had found some good friends and was enjoying himself. He was unhappy the last time he called me. He said he had been tricked."

"It wasn't us," Glenn said.

"I know," Jon said. "It was someone named Paulus and a woman he called a bitch. Dad never talked like that. He said he was going to set things right, but that was the day before the accident."

That confirmed my guess. Jon had discovered the fraud and was going after them. Jon didn't know how dangerous they were, and I was sure he hadn't figured out that Mrs. Carlisle's death was related to the fraud. He'd have called the police immediately if that had been the case.

"Your Dad and I were friends," Glenn said. "Will here had just come to work here, so they had just met. Your Dad was a good man. The residents just loved him."

"I'm following in his footsteps?" Jon asked. He smiled. "Maybe footsteps aren't the right word."

"Let's just say you share the same tastes as your father," I said. "I didn't know your father as well as Glenn, but you may be a bit more daring. He wasn't into fucking much."

"You never fucked him?" Jon asked looking at Glenn.

"Just once," Glenn said. "Two days before he died. It was his first time and he loved it."

"Am I like him?"

"You're identical." Glenn said. "You have the same tight hole. You react the same way." As he said that, Glenn rolled Jon over and slipped his cock into the boy's ass for the third time. This time he was very gentle. "You're feeling the same thing your Dad felt. He loved it too," Glenn continued. He slowly thrust his cock into the boy hole as I sucked Jon's cock. Each thrust pushed Jon closer to his next orgasm.

"Did you shoot in him?" Jon asked.

"I sure did," Glen said as rear loaded Jon's willing ass. Later Jon fucked Glenn. That was very good. Glenn fell asleep. In the middle of the night, Jon cuddled next to me. I got hard. That was what he wanted. He got my head at his hole tried to impale himself on it.

I used the lube on the bedside table to ease the way. My knob was in, but his body was putting up a fight. Next to the lube was a bottle of Rush. I told him to take a snort and see if it made it easier. Jon sort of melted on my cock. That little pink ass hole I had noticed several hours before we had now stretched to its limit. Jon was enjoying every inch of my cock. His moans woke Glenn. He impaled himself on Jon, so we formed another fucking trio.

Part II

We got Jon on the train first thing in the morning. I was sure he would sleep most of the way to Philadelphia. I made some calls and found Vince and the police were busy. They had search warrants ready to go and had R. Winston, Henry and Tiffany under 24 hour watch. They also had tapped their phones.

Glenn and I got back to Essex Park and found the Captain was stirring up the pot. He went to Tiffany and asked to rent the clubroom for his cocktail party. He told her about his guest of honor, Sir Frederick Harter. He told me she blanched when she heard his name. "I know this is very short notice, but Emily was my dear friend. She would have wanted this," he said.

The Captain hand delivered invitations to everyone, including the staff. He wanted to make sure everybody knew. The residents were all excited. After Jon's death, they needed a festive event. Most had seen him on PBS. Even those who didn't were pleased to have a genuine English Knight.

I got Gus to move in with Captain Green. I wanted some extra protection. He wasn't going to be alone in his house.

Sir Frederick did his part to increase the pressure on our suspects. He had been out of public view for a decade. He gave a major interview on the Today Show. He talked about modern art hoaxes and scams and described one similar to the Essex Park scheme. He also got a Katie Couric interview on the evening news.

The art historian was elderly, but handsome and authoritative. Katie asked him if he was involved in a case now. He said no, but with a slight hesitation. I admired the skill he showed. To most it was just a comment, but it should have scared shitless the guilty parties.

Joe and Roy were doing their own investigations. They moved in different circles from the police and Sir Frederick. Joe had decided the only way to save the reputation of Essex Park and his development company was to go all out helping. I told them of my conversation with Jon Jr. "He told his son that he had discovered something and was going to do something about it. My guess is he didn't know how far they would go. They killed him before he had a chance to turn them in," I said.

"He should have acted faster," Joe said.

"I don't think he was the kind of man who had encountered anything like that," I said. "He wasn't the suspicious type."

"Is our Knight going to be safe?" Joe asked.

"I have an extra man with him," I said. "Your security guys, The Fillmore Group, have their best people here. Billy Fillmore is loaded for bear. They drugged one of his guards and tried to blame the first death on her."

"How about the food? Is Essex Park catering the party?" Joe said. "They could slip him something."

"You are a suspicious guy!" I said. "The caterer is one of my friends. The waiters and several of the cooks are my operatives."

"The car?" Joe asked. He was thinking about Jon's "accident."

"I've hired a rental limo from Richmond," I said. Joe almost looked satisfied.

Two days later Captain and Gus went off to the Richmond Airport to pick up the elderly historian. The trap was set.

I was on grounds duty making sure the clubhouse and office areas were in condition suitable to receive Sir Frederick. Bill Davis was working on the other side of the building. Together we could see anyone who entered, or left the area. The residents were a twitter. Several ladies had gone off to Richmond to get new dresses. Ira was in charge of decorating the clubhouse. He was into flowers big time. He was hyperactive, so not a flower went into a vase he had not personally inspected and approved.

Sir Frederick arrived in the massive Limo and went to the Captain's house. He was to rest a while, then have a small dinner with the Captain, Gus, Joe, Mitch and Larry. Roy sent Henry and Tiffany home early. He told them they would be needed the next day for the party.

At 7:30, I got call from Vince. The wiretaps had paid off. One of the Essex Park resident's helpers called Henry. He gave him a report of the goings on at Essex Park. The man was a Pilipino named Gustavo. He was one of R. Winston's boys and apparently had been slipping information to Henry. He was the one who noticed I had been hanging around. Theoretically, he was a personal helper for a man who lived behind Mrs. Carlisle's house.

Fillmore Enterprises took care of him. They called him to the security office and turned him over to the police. Liz, the night guard took over taking care of the elderly gentleman. I later found out Henry called Gustavo at 10:30. Liz got the phone and said Gustavo had been taken sick and was off to the hospital. Henry was disappointed and agitated. He wanted to know which hospital, but Liz did her best "I know nothing" routine.

After dark, I went to the Captain's and met Sir Frederick. Gus had just completed giving him the rundown on the forged paintings. Sir Frederick was smaller in person than he was on television and he a quite pronounced Scots accent. He reminded me of a Scottish Terrier. Like the Terrier, he was a ratter, and Sir Frederick smelled a rat. His terrier like instincts was hidden under an affable and polite exterior. He was the kind of man I like to hire.

At 10:00, I got a call telling me a moving van had arrived at the Miller Galleries of Americana. Several men began to load the van as R. Winston loaded his car with personal luggage. He was going on a trip. The police moved in. His trip was to jail.

I spent the night at Essex Park. Glen had gone home, so I stayed with Mitch and Larry in their hotel room. I had nothing to do until the next morning. The police as well as the FBI and Immigration and Naturalization agents were hard at work. R. Winston was potentially the missing link in the *China Queen* mass murder. From what little I knew of R. Winston, I didn't think it wouldn't take much for him to spill the beans.

We were all tired. While I was always up for some fun, when I got on the bed, I fell asleep as soon as my head hit the pillow. Maybe Mitch and Larry had some fun, but I was dead to the world. I woke at 6:00 the next morning feeling good.

I went to the bathroom to shower. When I got out, I noticed the door to the adjoining suite was ajar. Joe and Roy were in that room. I heard some voices muttering, so I went in. Joe was on a cell phone talking with Billy Fillmore. Nothing unusual happened at Essex Park that night.

Roy came out of the bath and saw me. "I slept like a rock last night," he said. He came close to be and whispered. "I had no idea Mitch was part of the brotherhood." I nodded. "Joe's been holding out on me."

"He just found out last week," I said. "He was surprised too."

"Larry too?"

"We all share the same interests," I said.

"Are they into chicken, or do they like their meat aged?" Roy asked. We were both naked, and it was clear Roy was interested.

"As far as I can tell they're open minded," I said.

Roy reached over and stroked my cock. I wasn't as interested as he was, but with one or two strokes and we had reached parity. "Have you sampled them?" I just smiled. By that time, Mitch was awake and he came over to us. He saw our two half-erect cocks. That was all he needed to get excited. Joe finished his call and joined us.

"I smell hard cock!" Larry cried. He was still in bed, but he either could smell the erections, or had extra sensory perception.

"We don't have much time," Joe said. "We've got to get over to Essex Park."

"It doesn't take much time if you do it right," Larry said. He was out of the bed and fully erect. A good sense of purpose and a full erection can often carry the day. Roy dropped to his knees and sucked Larry and Mitch. Joe joined him on the floor and took care of me. In the spirit of fair play, we rotated partners. I noted that Mitch had a particularly good time with his uncle.

Larry broke the anal barrier. When everyone's sucking sometimes it's hard to switch. Larry wanted it bad. He was on the floor already; he got on his hands and knees and wiggled his ass to see who was interested.

Roy took the bait. Mitch got some lubricant and coated Roy's bloated member. Roy was careful. He made a little trial thrust into Larry rear. Larry opened wide and on the next thrust Roy's entire cock vanished into the love tunnel.

Roy's ass was open now. Joe winked at me, lubricated his meat and popped through Roy's sphincter. That too was easy. I had a feeling Joe's cock had a long time relationship with Roy's ass. I wondered if Larry was a good dancer; he sure had a good sense of rhythm. He easily adjusted his movements to the older men's thrusts.

Mitch and I were the odd men out. I sucked him and got a mouth full of the creamy white stuff in return. Mitch wasn't the strong silent type when it came to orgasms. His moans seem to have triggered Roy's climax. Roy was the silent type, but his body spasmed and twitched at each ejaculation. Since he was the filling in a fuck sandwich, both Larry and Joe popped.

We showered, dressed and got back to Essex Park in fifteen minutes. I still had a full load in my balls. Joe was concerned I was left out, but I told him they could draw straws for my cum later. He thought that was fair.

Much had gone on over the night. Liz, who had been the night guard who had been drugged on the night of Emily's death, knew all the residents. She knew which ones had helpers who might have been supplied by Henry, or R. Winston.

That morning, Billy's people had already checked them out as they came into work. They confronted one of them, a young Indonesian boy. He told all. His sexual experience with Henry had been bad, very bad. He had no hesitation giving details when Liz interrogated him. Liz said he was a nice boy and was deeply attached to the elderly couple he was helping. He was afraid they would make him swindle them. The boy had been told to tell them of a great art dealer. The Indonesian had no idea what that was about. He also knew who else was spying for Henry. Now we had them all.

Henry and Tiffany arrived at 9:00 and they looked uneasy. I couldn't tell if it was because of Sir Fredrick's cocktail party, or if they had realized something was going on. Essex Park had a dining room that was available to all the residents. The assisted living people were the regulars, but any resident could use it if they wished.

The Captain usually didn't use it, but today he appeared with Sir Frederick and Gus. Henry watched from the sidelines and was white as a sheet. The Captain played the role of a Lord Mayor squiring the Queen around an engagement. He made sure he talked to several of the people who had suspect paintings.

Gus impressed me. He was perfect as the Captain's nephew, but he also was watching everything. I was planting flowers on the terrace and several of Fillmore's people were nearby. Everyone wanted to glimpse Sir Frederick, so that didn't cause suspicion.

It was a beautiful day, sunny and warm. The gloom that had settled over Essex Park after Emily and Jon's deaths lifted. It had lifted for everyone except for Henry and Tiffany. They were cornered rats.

The caterers arrived. They were friends of mine, so I could feel safe. They set up the room with the efficiency of a military unit. By 4:30, they were ready. The party was to start at five. Ira came by with several buckets of additional flowers. He was worried some might have drooped during the day.

He was in the room for about five minutes when he came running out. "Someone has messed with my arrangement!" he screamed. You would have sworn someone had tried to kill him. I went in to see the offending flowers. It was at the main table where Sir Frederick was to stand.

"It's too tall! And it's drooping!" Ira complained. "I made it short so Sir Frederick wouldn't be dwarfed by it. It's a good foot taller."

Tim the caterer came out and said none of his people had touched it. It seemed comical, then a thought struck me. "Get it out of here!" I said. Roy was nearby and we carried it out of the room. I took it to the trash area to the side of the kitchen.

I took out the flowers. There was no water in the ornamental urn. There was a rectangle of plastic explosive and a cell phone operated detonator in the bottom of the vase. I had more experience with bombs than I wanted to have and I disconnected the detonator. To be safe we put it in the catering van and took it off the property. The police were waiting nearby. They took the device and monitored it for a call. Inside the room, Ira quickly arranged flowers in another urn and returned it to the room looking unchanged. I thought Ira would have been spooked by the bomb, but he was fine. A misplaced flower was a disaster; a bomb he could deal with.

I was wondering why Henry and Tiffany were still in their offices. Roy told me that they said they had to get some things done before the party. Guests began to arrive at five and the Captain, Gus and Sir Frederick came a few minutes later. All the public rooms of Essex Park had some security cameras. They were to see if anyone had a heart problem, or stroke when staff wasn't present. They fed into the main office and to the security office. Henry came over to the party, but Tiffany stayed in the office. Tiffany was watching the office monitors as Henry steered Sir Frederick toward the head table area. She hadn't noticed the maid cleaning up the office area. I had noticed Tiffany didn't worry about unimportant people. The maid didn't count.

When they reached the area next to the urn, Tiffany made a call. The cell phone rang in the van. I don't think Tiffany knew what hit her. Fillmore's security people got her and turned her over to the police. Roy asked Henry outside to talk about something. They arrested Henry as soon as he was out of sight.

The party was a great success.

Henry had no idea Tiffany was going to blow him up with Sir Frederick. He didn't take it well. R. Winston was more than willing to turn in Henry for the prostitution scheme and to turn in the "businessmen" behind the *China Queen* murders. Most of them were in China, but the Chinese government has no tendencies towards mercy.

The next few days were a confused series of interviews with local and federal agencies. The complex relationship between the art forgery and fraud and the prostitution-illegal immigration schemes puzzled the investigators. They were use to one, or the other. Vince was the one who seemed to get it all. He had been in on it from the murder of Mrs. Carlisle. It was established that Essex Park was not involved and Jon was murdered when he discovered the plot. Tiffany arranged the murder and fire. Henry had taken care of Jon. Jon had found him out and Henry was scared. Henry couldn't figure any way to get out of it without killing Jon.

I was afraid I would have to testify in court, but the entire case seemed to inspire mass confessions of the guilty parties. Two weeks later Sir Frederick exposed the scam on a 60 Minutes segment, but he kept my name out of it. Jon looked good, as did my client, Billy Fillmore. The Essex Park administration appeared to be serious and on the ball. It was good for everyone.

I went back to running Clydesdale and Company and fell into a slew of time-consuming cases. One of the strange things about my work is you can be 100% absorbed in a case, but when you crack it, it vanishes. A week later the Essex Park case seemed as if it had taken place years ago.

Two months later, I got a call from Larry. He was still running Essex Park until they could find a new permanent director. He said Joe and Mitch were coming to town and they wanted to thank my men and me. Joe had rented a house on the river and was going to have a party. I said that was fine with me.

"He will have Glenn and Bill Davis there. I was thinking you might bring Vince "Firehose" Desoto, Rick, Gus and Sedgwick to the ball," Larry said. "Joe told me he's going to be serving punch laced with Viagra. You get my drift?"

"You mean there's no need to over dress?" I asked.

"You got it," he replied. "There is no need to worry about drinking too much either. Plan to stay the night. He's providing lubricant and poppers." I sounded good to me. I knew Vince was always up for sexual romp, as was Rick. I told Gus about it, but he already knew. He was the Captain's date. I called Sedgwick and asked if he was interested.

"Are you asking me to an orgy?" he asked.

"That's the way it looks to me," I said.

"I think I'm too old and too ugly to do that."

"Take my word for it, you will do just fine," I said. "They aren't after beach bunnies and they like a man who has some mileage on him."

"Shit, I reached the retread stage," Sedgwick complained. "I've never done this before, but I'd love to try it."

A week later, I was in a van with Sedgwick, Vince and Rick heading to a house on the York River. It was gated, but when we drove up, the gate opened and we drove down a long, winding road through a wooded area and came up to an impressive modern mansion. We parked beside several other cars and Roy greeted us at the door. He was nude except for some leather accessories.

Mitch came over told us we could undress in a room to the side. He led us there, we stripped and he gave us a towel. We then went to a wing on the side of the house. It contained a luxurious indoor pool. There was a sling artfully erected in the corner of the space. The Captain, Gus and

Joe were talking. Larry, Bill, and Glenn entered. Much to my surprise Glenn was with Jon Jr. Jon was a good 20 years younger than most of the men, but that didn't bother him. Some of the men had been uneasy about his age, but Mitch carded him. He was 20. Jon had ways to make friends fast. We got a drink and made introductions. Roy was serving drinks.

As a group, we looked like a beach party movie that had aged, turned bald and gotten very hairy. It took no time at all for us to get comfortable. Sedgwick hit it off with Roy immediately. Sedgwick was an art historian, but he was all man. I think Roy liked the aging hippie types. Glenn had a tube of lubricant and he went around the room squirting it up any available ass. Glenn did Joe first. Joe bent over and spread his ass wide. That set a good example. No one seemed to object in the slightest.

It was a sex party so everyone knew the other guests were here for that purpose. It simplified the getting to know you part of the event. Rick was the first to suck. He took care of Mitch. Soon Larry and the Captain joined the mutual sucking society. I saw Joe get into the sling. Vince DeSoto noticed that too. Taking Vince's fire hose was a baptism of fire, but that didn't seem to bother either man. A small group gathered around the copulating men. I didn't know if they were there to watch, or were in line.

I got in the pool and swam a few laps. Gus, Bill Davis and Roy were in the water too. Gus and Bill were obviously friends now. Their landscaping interests weren't the only bond they had. Sedgwick sat on the edge of the pool. Roy started a conversation with him. That conversation was short. Roy wanted to taste the art historian's organ. Whatever oozed from Sedgwick's cock, Roy wanted.

I got out of the water and went over to the sling. The sling was a good conversation starter. Glenn was there to add lubricant when needed. Several times, he used his cock to get the lubricant deeper into Joe's ass. Vince had pulled out and Mitch was in his Uncle's ass. For his part, Joe was a good sport. He was clearly enjoying the event.

Mitch began to moan. He twitched and shivered as he ejaculated deep in Joe's ass. When Mitch pulled out Vince returned to the sperm lubricated hole. Vince must have gone a bit deeper because Joe's eyes crossed and he began to shoot. I was right next to him so I bent over and swallowed as much as I could from Joe's spewing cock. I had forgotten how good a twitching cock and fresh cum can be. We helped get Joe out of the sling.

I got in the sling next. I figured if Joe could open his ass for his men, I could do the same. Over the next half hour a Whitman's Sampler of cock types fucked me. The only common elements they shared was that they were all hard and their owners were enthusiastic.

Joe was the last one in line. He didn't want to fuck me, he was interested in the man-seed stew brewing in my ass. Had he possessed a straw, he'd have been a happy man. Joe had a long tongue. Jon was nice enough to help Joe. He slipped his cock into my ass, pulled it out and then let Joe lick the sperm stew from it. A friend of mine called that dip sticking. It was postgraduate level gay sex, so clearly Jon's days as a virgin were over. I was a little dizzy when I got out of the sling. A quick dip in the pool revived me. It was getting late and we had dinner on a terrace overlooking the river. It was beautiful.

Jon took my place in the sling. Larry was first in line. They formed a pretty couple. Jon's Dad took three cocks in his ass days before he died. Jon wanted to feel what his father felt. Larry was the last of us to fuck him.

At dinner, Vince and Joe filled us in on some of the missing pieces of the puzzle. The main scheme was the art swindle. A man named Newton Smith from New York ran this. He was a former employee of one of the big auction houses and used his connections to find likely marks. He had been R. Winston's lover, and was currently Tiffany's lover. He was open-minded when it came to sexual playmates. When Tiffany discovered Newton had been plowing other fields than hers, she went ballistic. The prosecutors loved that.

R. Winston and another former lover, Henry, developed the prostitution sideline. The boss man suspected something was up, and Tiffany went to Essex Manor to investigate. She found out about the prostitution scheme and discovered Henry was the man who forgot to pick up the container holding the Chinese men. Tiffany realized Newton would be in deep do-do if that came out.

Mrs. Carlisle told Henry about her party for Sir Frederick. He had no idea who Sir Frederick was, but Tiffany knew. Through the grapevine, Newton also found out the Chinese organization that sold the men to R. Winston, were unhappy about the deaths. Henry handled the purchase under an assumed name. Being caught by the Feds, or the State of Maryland was one thing. The Chinese criminal organization had a different interpretation of the phrase cruel and unusual.

Fortunately, that organization had no connections in rural Virginia. New York was a different matter. Newton and Tiffany were scared shitless. Emily had to die. Tiffany had access to the Chinese barbiturates and set the fire.

"The interrogators were shocked at both Henry and Tiffany's lack of remorse," Vince said. "When Henry admitted he forgot to get the men, it was as if he had forgotten to let the dog out. It didn't bother him one bit. Tiffany said Emily was old and going to die soon anyway."

"When Jon found out about the scam he had to die too?" Larry asked.

"He discovered the forged painting scam, but had no clue about the prostitution operations," Joe explained. "Henry tried to blackmail and then threatened him, but Jon wouldn't betray the people under his care. There were way too many dead people for Henry to take a chance. Jon had to go. Unfortunately for Henry, the 18 dead Chinese men were man slaughter, but Jon's death was murder in the first degree."

"There is no loyalty among thieves and once the plan began to come apart, everyone tried to implicate the other," Joe said. "The Chinese have arrested twenty or thirty people, we have about twenty, but that total is still rising."

After dinner, the party got a bit wild. Roy and I team fucked Sedgwick. Then I helped Roy discover how much he liked to bottom. Roy had a vision of the Virgin Mary while impaling himself on Vince's cock. That may well have been the first time that had ever happened to a Jew. His real name was Saul Meyer. From then on, the night turned into a haze of lust and passion.

Driving back to Richmond the next day, Rick told me I was the first person he had met who not only sleep walked, but also sleep fucked.

"Is that what happened?" I asked. "I was wondering how I got in your ass last night."

"It was hard for me to sleep with your cock in my ass," Rick said.

"Sorry about that," I said.

"Shit, it was the best night of my life!" he replied. I guess that's a sign of a good party.

About the Author

Bob Archman is a retired man living in rural Virginia. He has liked mysteries ever since he got his first Hardy Boy's book in 1957. He also likes Agatha Christie's mature detectives, Hercule Poirot and Jane Marple. He is interested in relationships between mature, hard working men. He tends to write about men who are actively engaged in their jobs and life and happen to be gay, rather than gay men who happen to have a job. A friend of his once asked, "Why be gay and not like sex?" Most of the men in Bob Archman's novels know the answer to that question.

Clydesdale
& COMPANY

A NOVEL BY
Bob Archman

CLYDESDALE & COMPANY

Clydesdale
GOES TO THE HUNT

A NOVEL BY
Bob Archman

A BONER BOOK

Clydesdale

GOES TO A FUNERAL

A NOVEL BY

Bob Archman

A
BONER
BOOK

Archman

CLYDESDALE GOES TO A FUNERAL

Clydesdale
GOES TO WASHINGTON

A NOVEL BY
Bob Archman

A
Bonsey
Book

Archman

The Cave of the Blue Bear

The Cave of the
Blue Bear

a novel by
Bob Archman

ARCHMAN

THE BUTLER & THE BARBARIANS

THE BUTLER &
THE BARBARIANS
BY BOB ARCHMAN

A
BONER
BOOK